DEATH

AT A

WEDDING

MARC WATSON

FLUKY FICTION
Newport, ME

Death at a Wedding

This book is a work of fiction. Names, characters, places, and incidents are either products of the author's imagination or are used fictitiously. Any resemblance to actual persons, living or dead, or actual events is purely coincidental.

ISBN: 978-1-7378944-4-5

www.flukyfiction.com

DEDICATION

For Patrick

I'll never be as good a writer, as good a creator, or as good a person as you were, but I'll never stop trying.
I owe you that.

Until we meet again

CHAPTER 1

The thought was repeating in his head over and over again. *This is not happening. This is not happening. This is not…*

"Kids, get inside!" he shouted, both of them crying and scared and confused. They were too young to understand what was going on. Why was Grandpa on the ground? What was Mom doing to his chest? Who was Grandma talking to on the phone in a panic? They had no idea. Everything was chaos.

The family had stepped out into the cold only moments before, looking to get some last-minute Christmas shopping in before the malls became complete zoos by mid-afternoon. Maybe they would swing by the food court. Both kids had made it clear they wanted burgers, fries, and some of that weird bubble tea Derek simply had no taste for.

It was while his mind was wrapped up in imagining the absolute grossness of one of those slimy balls in his mouth that Derek's father-in-law had complained of a bout of dizziness. Next thing anyone knew, he was on the ground unconscious.

His wife, bless her to the moon and back, was on it instantly. She was a personal trainer and had been involved with more than one similar incident at her gym. She had multiple levels of first aid training and knew what to do. But this wasn't some customer; it was her own father.

Even still, she reacted at once, taking his vitals and talking to him in a loud-but-firm voice. Janice was an unstoppable force of will most days. When they got into fights, he loathed that aspect of her. At a moment like this he wouldn't trade it for the world. It just may save her father.

Janice pumped away at her father's chest. Derek had never seen CPR chest compression in real life. He'd done his own first aid for work, but half-paying attention while pumping away on a plastic training dummy wasn't anything like the real thing when it's someone you love under your hands. That's the kind of thing no instructor in the world can adequately prepare you for.

It was as all of this was going on that he snapped back to reality; his mother-in-law, Joan, trying to get his attention. "Derek. Derek! Address?"

"What? Sorry, Mom. What was that?"

"Your address? The dispatcher needs it. I'm sorry, I don't remember it and they need it right away and I think…"

"Ok, ok Mom, sorry, yeah, of course… Kids, *please*! Give me a moment!" Both kids stopped crying, but were clearly about to let loose again. This shouldn't be happening at Christmas. Not to kids. Not to anyone. "Sorry, yeah, 7713 Norwood Drive." Joan repeated the address to the 911 operator, and then continued answering questions about her husband and what had happened.

Derek suddenly felt as useless as a shit-flavored lollipop. He had to collect himself. He had to help.

Janice kept working. She wasn't a big person, but as a trainer she was as strong as a bull; fit and disciplined. He thought about offering to switch out (How long had it been? One minute since he collapsed? Ten? He had no idea anymore), but she was a woman possessed, clearly fighting the urge to speed up. CPR had a rhythm, and you had to follow it for the best results. She would never accept his help, and he knew he wasn't as good at it as she was. She just kept working, looking into her father's glazed eyes, foam and saliva forming around his mouth while an ungodly sound came from his throat like someone was choking in the distance.

Derek turned back to the kids, their eyes wide as they watched their mom. He had to stop it. He had to get the image of what they were seeing out of their eyes. "Hey, I'm sorry I yelled, guys, but Mom needs to help Grandpa, and Grandma needs my help getting the doctors here…"

"Why does he need a doctor? What happened to him? I'm sorry I said I wanted to go to the mall!"

What? Oh, that's right, now he remembered: both kids started the talk about going. Joan and Janice seemed happy enough to oblige, and Derek was game (despite what seemed to be an ever-growing headache), but Hugh had protested (albeit only slightly; pleasing grandkids was his job, after all), wishing instead to have a seat in the living room and maybe take a nap, but eventually they were dressed and out the door. Now, all of this was happening.

Kids didn't understand this, though. Not when they were four. "No, no kiddo. This isn't anything you did. Don't you think that. This is just an accident, and we are trying to make it better. I promise I'll explain it all to you soon, but right now I need you both to go inside and wait for me to come get you. There's about to be doctors and ambulances and who knows what else, and they all want to help your Grandpa Hugh, but it will be easier if we get out of their way first."

"Derek? Derek!" It was his mother-in-law again. Her fear and panic looked to be taking over.

"Yeah, Mom?" he said, still looking at his kids and trying to shepherd them inside.

"It's the operator," she answered, voice quivering. "She has some questions. I don't know what an AED is and she wants to know if you have one?"

Ha, he *did* have one, but it was in his work truck back at the yard right now. It may as well have been on the moon for all the good that was going to do. "No, sorry Mom, tell them we don't have one here."

He looked back to see Joan's face drop, but to her credit she relayed the message without fail. Strong women bred strong daughters.

When he looked back, the kids had finally started to go inside as requested and Derek guided them, standing between them and the terrifying scene happening in the driveway. He got them in, closed the door, took a breath, and went once more unto the breach.

As he arrived back at the driveway, he was about to ask Janice if she needed his help when he saw the car pull up across the street and come to a sudden halt.

The car was an older black SUV or crossover or whatever they were called these days. Heavily tinted windows at first gave him hope that this was a police ghost car and they had come to help, but reality told him this wasn't the case. The car was too old, and dirty from slush and road salt. Ghost cars were usually newer and well-maintained.

The driver door opened, and Derek watched a man step out with measured caution, seemingly assessing the situation. Derek was simply thankful someone had stopped. Maybe they had a way to help he hadn't thought about. The man was slightly above average in height and didn't look terribly old. Younger than Derek was for sure. It was only as he stepped forward that something seemed off about him.

It was the ensemble he was wearing, Derek thought briefly. Black. Everything was black. Not all the same shade (because that would be weird) but similar. A long black wool winter coat over a black t-shirt, black jeans, and black winter hiking boots. A black beanie on his head, black fleece gloves on his hands, and black sport sunglasses with mirrored lenses on his face. It was odd, but nothing worth thinking about when an emergency was happening.

"Hey!" Derek shouted out as the man stepped forward. "Hey, do you have an AED or something? My father-in-law collapsed and I'm not sure when the paramedics will arrive." He looked at Joan hoping for an answer, but she was now over by Janice and Hugh, the cell phone in her hand. The operator was apparently relaying further instructions to his wife over speakerphone.

The man shook his head. "No, no I'm sorry, I don't. Not sure you'd be able to use one anyway. There's melting snow and ice everywhere."

Derek just noticed that now that the words had been spoken. It was true. Hugh had collapsed in an area with water all over the ground. No AED would help here. Not without moving him to someplace dry, and he seriously doubted Janice was going to allow that to happen. No, it was better to wait for the professionals.

As if on cue, sirens could now be heard in the distance. Help was on the way.

"Hey," the young man said, noticing the sirens as well. "There's some good news, eh? Is there anything I can do to help in the meantime? Does she need someone to step in? Is she getting tired?"

Derek shook his head. "No, no she's doing great. You're doing amazing, honey!" No response, not that he expected one. "Thank you so much for stopping. Help is coming, though. All we can do right now is pray."

The stranger's face twitched. "Yeah, sorry to say I'm not much for praying. But you know what? This close to Christmas, that's likely the least I can do, right? It's a time for miracles and all that."

Derek wasn't much of a spiritual person either, but he realized that every idle moment he'd had since Hugh went down had silently been filled with prayer to no god in particular. Just a wish into the ether since that was all he could really do right now. Was that what people meant when they said "thoughts and prayers" during a crisis? He had always bristled at what he considered apathy and a complete lack of action on the part of the person saying that kind of thing, but standing here with this man in black, watching his wife desperately try to save her father's life, and knowing there wasn't a damn thing he could do now that the kids were inside, he thought he finally understood it. Sure, most of those bullshit social media posts were hollow, but mixed in there were people who likely genuinely cared but were also powerless. Thoughts and prayers were literally all they had to offer in trying times. Derek had loathed them for so long, and now he felt guilty on top of a million other feelings.

"Hey, any idea what's going on? Did he just fall there or what?" the man in black asked.

"Yeah. We were just heading to the car and then he rolled to the ground."

"Oh jeez, that fucking sucks, man. I hope he's going to be ok."

Derek nodded. "Oh God, me too. He's such a great guy. Our kids are freaking out right now. They watched the whole thing happen. They must be so scared."

He wanted to step closer to his wife, offer kind words or support however he could. Or he should go to the kids, shouldn't he? He felt frozen in place. Was this shock? He didn't know. His legs felt weak, like they wouldn't take him somewhere even if he wanted to.

"Ah shit, kids saw this? God damn."

"I know. I know. I should go look after them. I feel pretty useless out here." The sirens were closer. It wouldn't be long now.

"Hey, so long as you got them out of the way and they're in the house they should be ok. Probably better to stay out here in case your wife needs you."

The man in black was right. Emergency responders were going to be here at any moment. He could look after the kids then. Right now, he needed to be present.

Good lord, the sounds coming from Hugh's mouth. No matter how this situation ended, that sound would haunt Derek.

The man in black took a step forward, seeming to try and find a better view of what was happening. Derek tried to follow but still couldn't move. Now that help was nearby and a faint hint of hope was growing, he was apparently giving into his shock.

The man in black stopped halfway between Derek and his wife, who was still pumping furiously but in proper rhythm with the voice on the phone. He shook his head once and turned around.

"God damn, man. What a fucking scene. Kids and grandparents and wives and you and soon there will be enough EMTs to look after an evening at Coachella. You gotta love Canada, right?"

Derek paused for a second, hypnotized by Janice. The conviction of her movements. The determination in her red, teary eyes. The repeated "Come on, Dad. Look at me! Come on. Come on..." She wasn't going to fail. She was an animal. She was never going to let her father slip away. As sure as he was standing there, Derek suddenly felt that although things would be very difficult, and the current Christmas season was basically ruined, they would persevere because his wife was a woman possessed. She could carry the load of the entire world right now if she needed to.

Derek faintly smiled. "I'm sorry, what's that about Canada?"

The man in black looked back at the scene. "I just mean your health care. Is it the best in the world? Hell no. But that ambulance, likely an EMT car, and maybe even a few fire trucks are about to pull up here and it won't cost you a god damned dime. I mean, I suppose that's true just about anywhere in the world, but if you just go a hundred miles south..."

Derek was distracted now, looking at the man with fresh, curious eyes. Was he a con man? An opportunist? A lawyer or something?

The man threw his hands up. "Sorry, sorry. I didn't mean to go off on a rant, especially at this moment. I just marvel at it. Two places so close yet lightyears apart, ya know? How a country so damn clean and nice could grow up and mature while it's attached to the hellacious shit-pile on the other side of the forty-ninth that tries to crush everyone and everything it touches. I know it's not all sunshine and poutine up here, but..."

"I'm sorry, but who are you? What are you talking about?"

The man faced Derek head-on, almost blocking what was happening. "Sorry again. I'm just... I'm a bit flustered. A lot of shit has happened lately and I'm having a tough time picking up the pieces. This whole thing, with the kids and the old man's heart attack..."

"We... We don't know what it is. It may not be a heart attack. Hugh is a very healthy guy."

The man tossed a skeptical look over his shoulder. "Clearly. Look, let's call a spade a spade here: all signs point to massive cardiac arrest. Let me guess: he was complaining about dizziness? Likely seemed a bit slow to move? I'd guess he wasn't a fan of going out to wherever you were off to. Wanted to have a seat or lay down or something?"

Derek's eyes blurred. "Yes. Yes, that's all true. How did you know that?"

"Uh-huh. Cardiac arrest, man. Take my word for it. I've seen it before. But gawd-damned is your wife doing her fucking best to not let him gently go into that good night, right? I mean, she is a keeper, no doubt about it."

Despite the confusion and the strange demeanor of the man, Derek smiled, finding a way to look past him and see his wife, her arms locked and hands interlaced, pumping her father's chest cavity with no signs of relenting, as if she could do this all day if she had to. She was amazing.

Derek was vaguely aware of the flashing lights, visible even in the bright daylight, and the flurry of people now milling around the two men standing in the driveway in a snowy suburban Canadian city. The professionals had arrived. Hugh was going to be ok. Derek knew it. He knew it in his heart.

The man in black stepped back beside him and put his arm around his shoulder. "Hey man, she did it. I mean, his chest will hurt like hell, and I expect months of recovery are just the beginning of his ordeal, but he'll make it. Hot shit, eh?"

"How long has it been since he fell?" Derek asked, confused. "I don't even know. It feels like forever. How can you say he will be alright?"

The man hugged Derek's shoulders. "Because I'm not here for him, man. I only have one passenger seat, and I'm really sorry to say it's just your size."

Tears began filling Derek's eyes as a stretcher wheeled past him in what seemed like slow motion. He looked into the reflection of the man's sunglasses, confusion giving way to understanding. Cold, horrible, terrifying understanding. "What… what do you mean?" He had to hear it. Had to understand fully.

"You know what I mean. And it's okay, right? God, please tell me it's okay. Tell me you get what's going on here. Don't… Derek, please, don't make me take you there… I'm so fucking tired…"

"How do you know my name? Are you…" He looked back at his wife, now leaning against the garage door, clearly exhausted, eyes still wide as she watched people load her father up, their questions flying and skilled hands doing what they did best. Derek's eyes met hers as she suddenly turned her head, looking for him. And then, he saw it.

All the fear, all the love, all the hope, all the sadness they had shared in their lives together poured from both of their eyes and filled one another with comfort.

"She… she's a hero," whispered Derek, a smile coming to his face.

The man nodded. "You're fucking right she is. More than you or I will ever be. She's a marble column holding up the god damn sky."

And then, Derek's legs left him completely. No longer just unable to move, now they couldn't even support his weight. As Hugh was now being pushed to the awaiting ambulance with Joan hustling alongside him, Janice stood up, desperate for her husband to hold her after what she had been through, what she had done. Desperate for the comfort he offered.

However, his arms didn't raise to meet her. Instead, she watched him fall to the ground.

The comforting arm of the man in black did all it could to make it a soft landing, but when someone went limp it was astonishing just how difficult maneuvering the human body could be.

Derek looked up once he hit the ground, at first confused, but then at peace. He was going to be okay. Just like Hugh before him, he was going to be fine. He knew this because Janice was there. Janice who could save lives. Janice who could hold up the sky.

Janice who could do it all, with or without him, just as he always knew she could.

Just as his wife's face came into view, blocking the light beyond, he could faintly hear the voice of the man in black say, "Thank fucking God," followed by the strange image of thousands of bright lights rising all around him like fireflies. And then, peace.

The man in black stepped back, immense relief on his face. Jesus Christ, that was a close one. It was already hard enough, what with the father-in-law and the kids around, and for fuck's sake it was almost Christmas!

The wife didn't even look at him. She just went from one disaster to another, and before the man had returned to his car he saw her scream for help. Even with paramedics and EMTs only steps away, it would never arrive in time. Derek was already gone.

Death was never fair. Death was balanced. Death was always where and when it needed to be, even if that meant taking a father from his young children because of an undetected brain aneurysm days before what should be the happiest day of the year, a day likely ruined for everyone involved here today for the rest of their lives. Even if it meant giving a handful of good, decent people the worst day of their lives for no great, grand reason whatsoever, Death was always where it needed to be.

He couldn't do anything about that. Not today. Not ever again. For now, all he could do was get into his car and drive away into the light. "Thoughts and prayers, Derek," the man sighed. "Thoughts and prayers."

CHAPTER 2

Ethan sat behind the wheel of the phantasmic car driving both down the road and into the void of space simultaneously. Before, when he had first taken this job, moments like this had threatened to pull his mind apart. He wasn't just in two places at once; he was literally everywhere. As time went on, his mind accepted it more and more. Now it was barely a distraction.

Lately, after what he had begun to refer to as "The Douchebag Debacle", he found himself coming back here more and more, into his own actual time and place, in order to settle his mind. A chance to reside in his own body for a bit before he had to re-focus on his job.

Ethan Dessier had been Death for almost two years in his own time at this point. He could only quantify it as "his own time" because in all of his travels through the infinitude of space, he'd come across worlds where things had slowed to a crawl and time almost dripped from the clock, and he had also been places that were here and then gone in the blink of an eye; a universe born, thriving, and then dead all before one could even say it had existed.

This place, however, was the most real to him. No other in all existence felt like this one did. This was where he came from, and this was where he belonged.

He focused on the road as opposed to the bright light of infinity, driving down the snowy Canadian streets, heading off for nowhere in particular. He had just dodged a bullet back there, and he wasn't in much of a rush to get back to work whole-hog.

He had just taken a loving young husband and father away from his family. A good man. A man with no deep secrets. He'd almost say a boring man honestly, but wasn't boring okay these days? People who kept their nose clean? Didn't cheat on their taxes? Told people when they dropped a five-dollar bill as opposed to taking it for themselves? That was who that Derek guy was, and now he was gone. Dead to the world; his essence, his "soul", already fractured into the sprawling kaleidoscope of everything, a million lights drifting into the rainbow that made up life itself.

God, how he fucking hated it. Still, it was better than the alternative. A fate that guy had just narrowly avoided.

His predecessor, a smart-ass squirrel who had been Death before him, had shown Ethan the expanse of everything when they were trying to convince Ethan to take the job (not that he had a choice in the matter, Ethan would later realize). Instead of easing him into it, Death had slammed Ethan with the light of infinity all at once, basically overloading Ethan's pitiful human mind until it burst and he passed out. Despite how glorious and awe-inspiring the actual light of everything was, a part of him always remembered that moment when Death assaulted his senses with it, effectively tarnishing the glory for all eternity. It was hard to fully appreciate something when your first experience with it had been so negative.

The miles (kilometers? He was in Canada after all) fell behind him as he drove, his human mind wrapped up in what had just transpired. Derek didn't deserve it, but if everyone who didn't deserve to die actually got to live, Death wouldn't have much of a job. It was a pleasant fact that most things could be considered "good" in the eyes of the masses, or at least "reasonably neutral". It was a part of the job Ethan had to get his head around very quickly. The hazard of being alive while in the role. The emotional impact of helping good lifeforms pass away.

Death, that is to say his predecessor, had no idea what remaining alive would do to Ethan when he took over. It was all new. Before, something had to die to become Death, its essence then entering the role briefly before passing on the role and then spreading itself back into the light. It was an effective system that had existed since the beginning of all time everywhere.

And then Ethan came along and fucked the whole thing up. Typical.

No plane crash could kill him. No existential dread could force him to off himself. No grand and deep understanding of the needs of the universe could convince him to shed his mortal coil for the greater good. And in the end, Death had agreed, and Ethan became a living Death.

And now, driving down another faceless suburban road, Death had to admit the truth.

He was so. Damned. Tired.

It had only been a couple of years, but mentally it had been lifetimes. A lifetime of lifetimes, really. Lifetimes of things dying. Every day, all day, an infinite number of times a day, death. How much death could the human brain stand? Ethan thought that he was beginning to find out.

But that wasn't even the worst of it. On top of everything else was the mess made by the aforementioned douchebag. The jerk who had cast him into this downward spiral. And for what? Just because his fucking ego was too big to admit defeat? Just because he thought *he* could dictate when someone was allowed to die? That wasn't the way the universe worked!

Ethan had been "hired" as Death to look after one particular problem child. A man (*and of course it was a human*, he thought) from a world where mankind had evolved what could only be described as superpowers by unlocking the potential of both the human mind as well as the universe itself. He had become too powerful, and his body and mind had collected too much of the essence of life to be considered safe. A man who had dodged death like a politician did the Vietnam draft. Ethan had been brought in specifically to stop him. To convince him not to do something terrible to his world. To prevent a catastrophe from happening that would have been so big it would ripple throughout the cosmos and threaten to end all life everywhere.

And Ethan had failed.

Not only had he failed, he failed as only he could: spectacularly. Failed on a level so monumental that only he had the brain expansive enough to appreciate how laughably horrible he had fucked up.

Death wasn't supposed to fail. Death did its job perfectly, and had for all of time. That was, until Death had chosen Ethan to take over and Ethan didn't die. From that moment, the failures mounted until they burst.

Life had once been so simple. Terrible, mind you, but simple. Now he had been to worlds with superpowered people, or worlds with feline overlords who oppressed dog-slaves, or a world where the only living things were various forms of grass. Ethan didn't think it was possible for a simple blade of grass to be an asshole on his level, but there was this one…

And here he was now, spiritually spread throughout everything, taking lives and distributing the pieces they left behind (only now the whole system still threatened to collapse under the weight of his monumental screw-up in another world), while physically and consciously he was here, in his own world, killing people like Derek and ruining his kids' and wife's lives as only death can.

For some time after he took the role of Death, while he was still getting his feet wet, he had kept a pretty tight grip on his presence in this reality. He had maintained his apartment with his roommate Tony back in Seattle, though he had quit his job. Why keep up that charade when he had a new position that consumed his every waking moment (and the fact that he soon had millions of dollars paid by the airline didn't hurt)? He kept his shitty car and his cell phone plan and had closer contact with his sister Arlene. He even went on a date with the photocopy girl Amy (she was actually an Administrative Assistant, but the fucked-up part of his brain that would always be an uneducated, serially abused basket-case would always think of her with that dismissive, sexist moniker no matter how hard he tried), and although they had a good time, it never turned into anything. It was a great night with reasonable (or at least passible) base-rounding later in the night, but that was it. Even as an omniscient god-figure, Ethan was still Ethan, a fact that worked against his modest libido at every turn.

He even stoked small fires under the cult-like following his lone survival of the plane crash dubbed the *Puget Plunge (* - Copyright dissolved due to lack of usage) had garnered. In some places they still had web pages dedicated to him, though most had moved on to including other survivors and mock-Christ figures as well as himself. Being the lone survivor of a massive plane crash was a fleeting celebrity, but what tiny pockets still remained after two years that did remember him made him smile.

No one was camped outside his door anymore, which made sense because he didn't have a door to camp on. After a few months of holding this part of his life as closely as he could, Ethan decided to fully embrace his role of Death. He thanked Tony for everything, gave him a bullshit excuse that he was moving to some fancy house in California with the airline settlement money, told his sister he was going to take the job he had lied to her about not taking months before, which gave him the ability to go quiet for long periods of time. And then Ethan just let go, drifting off into the empyrean. Ever since then, he didn't have much time for his "real" life.

Things were darker now. Out there somewhere the universes still threatened to tear themselves apart because of him, and he was fighting desperately to stop it. He'd already failed once. That meant he could fail again. Death was no longer a passive entity with a single purpose and no say. Being alive meant he now had some autonomy over the job, an autonomy he had used to try and best the douchebag in a battle of wits and will, but having a choice meant having the ability to make the wrong choice, and that was what had happened.

The details weren't important anymore. All that mattered was that he had failed, and now he was back, driving a ghostly, conjured replica of his mother's old car (was it a station wagon? Jesus, the mid-aughts were just horrible for vehicle design experimentation) through the streets, going nowhere in particular, desperately trying to shut off the part of his existence that wasn't here, and was out there claiming souls like cheap baseball cards to stick in the spokes of existence.

It just hurt so god damned much...

A cold truth came to him in the months after he had taken the job. His predecessor, the squirrel that would be Death, had explained things about the job and the worlds that relied on it likely better than anyone could have hoped, but eventually Ethan began to realize that Death had skipped a key detail: how to quit.

Up until Ethan, the role of Death had been very temporary for those that held it. Days, hours, or just minutes were all that were usually spent on the job. Nothing had even come close to being Death as long as Ethan was now. Couple this with the fact that he was still alive, and even aging, meant that there was no playbook for what came next. Was he stuck in the role until he died of old age? Or killed himself? That would be a sick joke, since that's exactly what the previous Death had been trying to get him to do all along. Maybe they would finally get their wish?

Fucking squirrels.

At first it hadn't really bothered him. Ethan just assumed the universe would tell him it was time, and give him someone to pass the role to. Maybe it was a sloth from the universe where dinosaurs never went extinct, or a dinosaur itself from a world that blinked in and out of existence in a heartbeat. Who said it had to be an animal? Ethan had met many noble and dignified plants, mushrooms, and microscopic lifeforms. His encyclopedic memory of all of the Deaths who had come before him said it was possible, but a series of fungi had been presiding as Death over the Permian-Triassic extinction event two hundred and fifty-ish million years prior, and very few had held the role since then. Who knew mushrooms were so good at handling events like The Great Dying? Ethan figured that when the time came, if he had to hand the job to a portobello, the shiitake was about to hit the fan.

Would it be as bad as his screw-up? Not a chance, but what did that say about him? Was Ethan just as important as fungus? What a cheery thought.

After the disaster in another world, Ethan had really begun to think about how long he was meant to go on. Maybe his desire to stay alive had broken the system and he was locked in some weird loop. A terrifying thought. What if he committed suicide after driving himself crazy and just POOF, he was Death again, only without any of his much-loved autonomy? As he tried to put the pieces of the heavens back together again, he figured he had no choice but to soldier on. If he failed, everything would collapse and end anyway, so it was either shit or get crushed by the giant shit-pot. Getting off didn't seem to be an option.

Lately he had been in a bit of a daze. Going about his galactic business almost like a drone. He had also started to take a more human approach to situations like the one he had just come from. He wasn't sure, but the initial results were promising, and showed that when he did step in, the odds of having to send someone Beneath went way down.

Lord how he hated Beneath.

Beneath wasn't Hell, at least not in the traditional sense of the word. There was no Heaven or Hell. (Thank God. God? Two years later and the nomenclature was still murky.) Everything that died simply went to where it belonged in the cosmic rainbow of Everything. It didn't matter if you were the Pope or a politician. All that mattered was that you were dead.

Some things had a really hard time letting go, though. A lot of things, actually. A disturbing number of things. Death came when you were prepared for it to happen, even if you didn't really want it to. You had to be "ready" to die. And most things were.

Some things, though. Things like, oh, say, Ethan's own drug-addled abusive mother, had to spend a bit of time in reflection. A sort of limbo or purgatory of their own creation. Some were quite nice, with the residents enjoying their time there, oblivious to the fact that they were actually dead. Just living peaceful normal lives until they realized what was happening, embraced death, and left.

Most were not so cheery. His mother, for example, had died of an overdose alone and abandoned, lost in a haze of booze and drugs and mountains of regret about how she had lived her life and what kind of mother she had been. Even now, she sat alone in an abandoned, derelict warehouse, nothing but bad memories and blueberry muffins to keep her company. Ethan wondered if she would ever leave that place. The last Death said that eventually everybody always leaves, but again the details were vague. Some were only moments, and some had been millennia.

Ethan had been to visit his mom a few times, outside of his first going there when he was "interviewing" for the job. His anger at who and what she was never went away, but more and more pity grew in his guts the more he saw her. She had not been a good person, and he wasn't the forgiving kind, but you couldn't choose family. He kept going back, and he kept regretting it. He never tried to save her though. He never tried to guide her towards the exit. He knew, as a veteran of this job now, that she must do it herself. Besides, he wasn't sure he'd help her if she wanted it. There was a guilty, deplorable part of his human side that felt that she was finally getting what she deserved for what she did to her kids. To him. Whenever he felt pity, he was flooded with memories of being woken up at the age of thirteen to her trying to smash in the back door because she'd left her keys somewhere horrible, had him drag her in and get her to bed, and her yelling at him for some fucking reason he didn't need to hear about while she stumbled around their house. The moments he woke up with her slouched shadow looming over him slurring words, or worse, saying nothing. Just staring. Maybe a bottle in her hand. Maybe drugs. Maybe…

Maybe…

Fuck! Snap out of it, Ethan. It was so easy to go back into those dark places when he was residing in his more human form.

Anyway, Beneath, as he'd come to call it, was not a place he wanted to put anyone or anything. It was part of the job, but when you could see into what could be called something's "soul" and it was good and decent and didn't deserve to be locked away for any length of time, having to do just that killed him.

So when he came to Derek and saw it was his time, but the situation around him was so chaotic and was hurting so many people he loved and who loved him, and a small part of Ethan felt that Derek wasn't willing to let go yet, Ethan stepped in before the moment happened. He helped Derek see that his wife was amazing and strong, and could carry on without him, although it would be difficult, so when the aneurysm took him, he was comfortable letting go. It was close though. Too close.

Ethan drove, pulling onto the highway and heading south out of the city, all the while trying his best to just get lost; either on the roads or in his own mind, he didn't care.

And then the phone rang.

CHAPTER 3

Ethan had almost forgotten he still had a cell phone. A holdover from days he took pleasure in turning it off and avoiding people. It snapped his mind to the here-and-now and he looked at the dashboard as the name popped up on the Bluetooth stereo.

He smiled. Of course. Who else could it be.

He pressed the "answer" button. "Hey sis. How's the Windy City?"

Arlene's voice was much more chipper than his was. "Windy, dumbass. Same as always. Windy and cold and stupid."

"So go buy a thick pizza."

"Sure, I'll grab one along with a book about Chicago clichés and why they suck." Her tone shifted to something less sibling-confrontational. "How are you doing?"

Ethan considered lying. Thought better of it. "I've been better, Arlene. Work has been... difficult."

"Has your boss been an asshole? He looked like an asshole. What was his name?"

Ethan had a sudden vivid memory of Death's smiling, idiotic face on the fake business card he'd handed her when he was convincing her of this imaginary think-tank job. "Pana," Ethan answered. "Azreal Pana, and no, he's fine. He's an asshole, you're right, but fine. He never bothers me. Besides, lately I've mostly been off on my own. I just had a really big business venture go rocketing south. It was pretty fucked up."

"How far south?" Genuine concern in her voice. It was baffling that these two had been spawned from the same place.

"Hades far, Arlene. *Way* down there. Far enough that I'd really prefer not to talk about it."

Silence for a moment. "That bad, huh? It's not like you to let work get to you that badly."

Wasn't that the truth. He had to change the subject. "Hey, what's up? Random calls aren't your style, and Mom can't die again, so what's up? Marriage or pregnant."

Arlene didn't miss a beat. "Marriage."

It was Ethan's turn to be silent for a second. "Wait... what? Really?"

The cheerier tone returned to her voice. "Yeah! Matthew proposed Saturday night! I've just been so wrapped up in everything I didn't call yet. Can you believe it!"

"No, I honestly can't," he answered, her obvious happiness infectious. "You mean you actually tricked him into a ring? What's the scam?"

"Oh fuck you, Ethan. The 'scam' is love..."

"Tell me about it."

An exasperated sigh on the other end of the line. "Look, seriously, he proposed on the Skydeck of the Willis Tower after dinner at the Metropolitan Club. I thought it was a work function, but he set it up with our friends! They all knew about it and we had a great night and... just... wow! It was amazing!"

"The Skydeck of the Sears Tower? What were you saying about clichés?" No force in all the universes would ever make Ethan stop saying "Sears Tower".

"Yeah yeah, I know, but whatever. Anyway, I wanted to call and tell you, but also ask you something."

He was genuinely curious by now. "Fire away."

"Well, we agreed we don't want a big wedding. Friends. Immediate family. Justice of the Peace. That kind of thing."

"Good. It'd be kinda hard filling out our side of the aisle." The

Dessier siblings didn't have any other real family. Since Arlene was a fair bit nicer than Ethan, he was sure she had a bunch of friends, but the family tree was basically barren.

"No kidding. Anyway, he'll be taking a job in Texas in the fall, so we wanted to get it done before we had to move. We're getting married in July. Quick ceremony. Probably dinner and dance and that's all."

Ethan's eyes went wide. "July? Jeez, you're not wasting time." Although it was quick, Ethan had no real issue once he thought about it. She was a grown-ass woman. She could do whatever the hell she wanted. She was usually right anyway.

"No, we're not. We want it done while we're still here with our friends and so they don't have to fly somewhere."

Ethan snorted. "Huh. It's a rich crowd, Arlene. I'm sure they wouldn't mind." Arlene had slowly climbed the ranks of her job (despite having to take off twice on no notice when Ethan had been in his crash). She wasn't doing too poorly herself, he was sure. It likely wasn't "airline settlement for dropping a plane on your head" money, but it wasn't nothing.

"Maybe," she answered, "but I didn't feel right about it. We both want a small wedding, so this is what we're doing." She would always be a humble girl. It made Ethan feel at ease, knowing how grounded she was. "Anyway, what I wanted to ask you was… and don't think this is stupid or lame or childish or…"

"Alright, alright," he interrupted. "I'll be your ring bearer. I demand only the finest of pastel tuxedos and the fluffiest of pillows, though, and I get to keep the pillow when it's over…"

"Ethan, I want you to give me away."

Dead silence from the car. The normally verbose and whip-smart Ethan was completely dumbstruck into total wordlessness. There was no Ethan-As-Death at that moment, only Ethan: the loner brother to a sister who was too nice to have any reason to be related to him.

"Yeah," she said quietly, "I'll give you a sec." Credit where it was due, she knew when to shut up and let a moment simmer.

He had no idea how much time passed before he spoke again, and that had nothing to do with his admittedly loose grasp on time and reality at any one passing moment. Finally, a sound escaped his lips.

"I… buh… ghah?"

Arlene actually laughed. "Wow. Very eloquent. And you say you're a communicator for a living these days?"

Ethan regained himself. "I'm sorry, but you made it sound all low-key and informal. Why the traditional part? A part that you think should involve me, of all people?"

"Well, we agreed to a small wedding party, and to do away with most of the modern wedding trapping bullshit, but… I don't know. I can't explain it. I know I want you there, and we're all each other really has left. Also, there's not much chance Dad will materialize out of thin air to do the job, not that either of us would want him to. One of us would likely murder him, and that's a great way to ruin a wedding."

Ethan's eyes narrowed at the thought of their father. *Ha*, he thought, *I know something you don't know…*

"Ok," Ethan finally replied, "but why me for that role? How many women are given away by their younger brother?"

"Only the coolest ones. Look, this is clearly non-traditional as fuck, but as my only actual relative worth mentioning, I want you involved. Not to try and tug your heartstrings or anything, but you're all I got. It's just a bonus that I don't hate you on any serious level. Besides, you owe me. I almost lost my job flying across the country to babysit you."

"Owe you? A plane landed on me, Arlene. A fucking plane! Besides, I bought you your condo, didn't I?" A gift with his excess of riches. Hell, he didn't need it.

"Loaned," she clarified. "You loaned me the money to get it. A loan I'm happy to pay back any time you ask." Ha, not likely. Not that she couldn't, but she was right; he did feel somewhat indebted to her for being there for him. He honestly felt it was the least that he could do.

The highway ahead stretched out south, nothing but snowy fields and intermittent cars. The perfect place to get lost in thought. "So, what would this regal position involve? What do you need from me?"

"Is that a yes?"

"No, it's a question, stupid. How much of my precious time do I need to dedicate to this? Do you want me to help pick cutlery and whatever? Or do I just roll up on the day of with a limo full of doves and strut over, give him some cheesy relationship advice, hand you over to him, and then get tanked and fuck a bridesmaid? I just want to be prepared."

"Oh fuck you, like any of my friends would ever touch you."

Ethan smiled. "A young, healthy, rich, well-employed gadabout like myself? Who's fooling who here."

"My friends are smart enough to see you for what you are, Ethan."

His heart fluttered and bounced for a moment. "Which is?"

A beat, and then the cold truth even he couldn't deny about himself. "An asshole. An undiluted, irredeemable asshole. God damn pure, Columbian high-grade shit."

Ethan actually laughed. "You got me. You're right. Can you believe I almost forgot about that little fact? Ok, so yeah, anyway, what would you need from me?"

Arlene's mood brightened again. "Um, honestly, whatever you're willing to give. I know you're busy with your stink bank or whatever, and most of the finer details have been worked out already, but there are still some things. I'd like a guy's eyes on dress choices, even if that guy is you. Maybe just be available for a call or Facetime if I need advice on something. Matthew and I were hoping to have an engagement party soon, after the holidays, so if you're free to swing by Chicago that would be great? I know you play fast and loose with your schedule."

Her gift for understatement was uncanny, even when she didn't know it. "I can likely squeeze you in. Did you know the airline gave me a lifetime travel voucher? What kind of ironic, tasteless bullshit is that! Anything else?"

"No, not really," she answered. "Try not to look like a homeless person on the day of, walk me down the aisle, maybe say a word or two at dinner?"

"Ha!"

"Okay, okay, a bridge too far, but we can cover that closer to the day," she relented. "Just, I dunno, be yourself, but maybe dialed back? Like, seventy-seven percent of yourself."

"Eighty-two," he countered.

"Eighty, and no jeans."

"I don't own anything else." That was true, regardless of world or reality.

"Okay, eighty, and maybe I get to take you shopping for a reasonable fucking wardrobe for the occasion, you skinflinty bastard. I'll even pay."

He knew her better than that. "No you won't. Liar."

"No, I won't. But maybe you'd actually enjoy it."

"What about our mutual history makes you think I would enjoy that, Arlene?"

Her smile could be heard over the phone. "Nothing at all. In fact, I'd bet you'd hate it, but I'd enjoy it and that's more important."

"Hey, you're the one asking me for a favor." How did she do that? How did she constantly twist the situation to make it sound like she was owed a favor? Although he would never, ever dare to say the words aloud, he realized there was more of their pleading, manipulative mother in her than she would ever admit.

"Making you dress nice instead of a high school dropout living on minimum wage is a favor to the *world*, Ethan."

Although it was said in jest, that one stung more than Arlene intended. Although he was going through a rough home life, and Arlene had long since abandoned them in an effort to save her mind and soul, Ethan was still very proud of the fact that despite all the shit his mother put him through he had graduated high school. He wasn't a great student, but he had passed.

His mother had torn up his diploma in a drugged-out rage, screaming, "This isn't shit! You aren't shit! The world doesn't give a sweet fuck about us! You think a piece of paper makes you worth something?!" and then she proceeded to throw the bits into the toilet and started undoing her pants. Ethan ran from the scene before whatever happened next.

The saddest part was, on a very visceral level, he agreed with her. A diploma didn't make you a good person. It didn't make the world care about you.

He suddenly thought of Derek, the man whose death likely ruined Christmas. Did Derek have a diploma? Probably. But he was also surrounded by family that loved him at the moment he died. Those two things were completely unrelated. As was sometimes the case, his mother had stumbled onto a great life-truth once again.

The bitch.

Figuring the silence had gone on too long to be comfortable, Ethan bounced back. "Fine. You have a deal. But that's a *hard* eighty percent, Arlene. I'm planning on milking every percentage point I can out of it."

"I'd be surprised if you didn't. And the engagement party?"

He mulled it over in his head. Death was everywhere, always and forever, so Death could likely be in Illinois in a few weeks. "I can make it work. Just let me know what you're thinking."

"Is the first weekend in January too soon? I only ask because there's an opening at the place we like and if we don't get it today it could be another few weeks..." Jeez, was she actually getting flustered? It's amazing what weddings, or even just the pageantry that led to them, could do to a person.

"Yeah, yeah, that's fine," he cut her off. "I can swing it. Give me the date and time and whatever and I'll be there. We can make it a whole... thing, I guess. Iron out the details of July while I'm there. But you owe *me* now. Making me come to Chicago in January borders on being a war crime in some countries."

There was genuine relief in her voice now. "So you'll do it? Come to Chicago? Help us out? Get involved? All that other shit you hate? Then walk me down the proverbial aisle?"

Ethan gripped both hands on the wheel in an attempt to settle himself before speaking. Sarcasm came so naturally to him that he was afraid it would ooze into his answer if he didn't fight it with everything he had. She deserved as much sincerity as he had to give, though it was still likely a miniscule amount.

"Arlene, Death himself could not stop me."

CHAPTER 4

There was no rationale that could be given as to why he made the choice he did that Saturday morning on the first weekend of January. He didn't need to do it. Hell, he didn't even *want* to do it, but for reasons only known to whatever god may exist (and as he was basically a god himself, Ethan felt very confident saying there was none), that morning Ethan found himself boarding a plane at SeaTac and flying back to Chicago.

He hadn't even touched a plane in a non-professional role since that horrible day, but as the days passed after he spoke with Arlene about her pending nuptials, he had realized that he enjoyed the sudden thought of a real-life goal. His mind had been so enthralled with speaking to her and actually doing something fun while not acting as Death that he couldn't help but get wrapped up in the moment. Once she had sent him the details of the engagement dinner with the explicit warning of "the eighty percent starts *now!*" he knew that this was something he honestly wanted to do.

He had spent the rest of the Christmas season spending more and more time in his regular human body, making sure to try and weed out as much of the craziness of his job as he could. At all times a near-infinite amount of death was happening, and in the background there was the ever-creeping feeling that the system of light and balance was slowly being unraveled, but for a few glorious moments every day, Ethan was just Ethan again. His subconscious went on autopilot and he just existed, with the chill of the wet air and the smell of life around

DEATH AT A WEDDING

him.

Everything great about life disappeared when he got on the plane.

Perhaps it was hubris to assume he could handle it. He could bend reality. He was literally the gatekeeper of the afterlife. Even as lowly Ethan, he figured he could overcome a minor thing like PTSD.

Nope. It was four hours of pure torture, despite being in first-class (if the airline was going to pay for him, they were going to pay *big*). Every creak of the plane as it moved. Every sound he deemed out of the ordinary. Even the sudden startle he got when the flight attendant came around asking what he would like to drink. It was all horrible.

At one point he thought it would be good to head to the bathroom and try to piss the fear away. But there, on the wall over the comically small sink, was the dispenser filled with boring, unscented, innocuous soap.

Due to the head trauma, Ethan had very little memory of the crash that killed everyone but himself. However, he very clearly remembered being rescued from atop a piece of flotsam while covered in this same soap. It had likely saved his life (well, that and an unimaginable will to live, according to his predecessor) but just looking at that jizz-white ooze in the container sent Ethan's head spiraling.

He could have beamed out any time he wished. He had the ability to just disappear and float off into the nothing without a care. The airline may ask questions about why someone was missing, but he was certain they didn't give a shit about him anyway. They'd paid him his money and given him his free pass. Hell, he had no doubt that as far as they were concerned, they felt they were even with him now. Or even worse: he owed them! Money can't replace trauma, and no one could tell him otherwise. Hell, he could also stretch his cosmic fingers to see if the plane had any sense of impending doom. Then he wouldn't need to be putting himself through this torture. But, no matter how he swung it, the human side of him wanted to get through this on his own.

Ethan endured. For Arlene, and also to try and stay normal during his interactions with her. He could do it. He needed this bit of mental self-flagellation to get into the zone, so he got back to his seat, ordered a complimentary glass of water (*God, how I wish I was a drinker…*) and did what he had to do. Once or twice, he would lay back and allow his mind to embrace his job. In the span of a few seconds, he could feel the glory of the all and everything, as well as the whisper of the void, the nothingness that sat opposite the light. That same nothingness that threatened to swallow all life everywhere if Ethan wasn't careful and kept fighting to fix his stupid mistake. Not a single soul on this airplane knew what could await them if the slumped, boring twenty-something in seat 3F didn't keep fighting back. No pressure.

The flight landed at O'Hare right on time just after lunch. If he wasn't so busy battling a horrible aviation-related mental trauma, Ethan likely would have said it was a perfectly uneventful flight. Still, he wasn't in a rush to jump back into one of those damned flying cylinders.

As he deplaned (*George Carlin was right, that is a fucking stupid word*), one of the flight attendants motioned to him specifically. "We hope you enjoyed your flight, Mr. Dessier. We look forward to continuing to have you join us."

Ethan withheld a snarl. "Oh yeah, thanks for not almost killing me this time." The attendant's smile faded quickly. Most people weren't prepared for maximum Ethan. He couldn't let it rest though. The stupidity of the sentiment needed to be called out. He turned to the old woman in the line behind him. "It's true, you know. Last time I flew with them I nearly fuckin' died. True story. You ever heard of the Puget Plunge? Well, funny story…"

"Mr. Dessier," the attendant intervened, smile forced on her face, "I'm sure you have someplace important to be. I apologize if I misspoke. We just wanted to say we are happy to see you again."

"No, your bosses just want to say how glad they are that all is forgiven. Ho-hum, life is back to normal. I'm only here because you gave me free tickets for life, and the settlement wasn't big enough for me to buy my own private train. Now, as you said, I'm off to someplace important. I'll see you when I want to relive the worst moment of my life again." Then, much like the man in black he'd taken the job of Death from shortly after they met in this very airport, off Ethan disappeared into the bowels of O'Hare.

Even in the cab ride downtown, Ethan fought to keep his mind on the here-and-now. The driver tried engaging him in small talk, but it became very clear that his fare wasn't chatty.

Ethan checked into his hotel not far from the river and messaged his sister that he made it in fine, and he would see them later that night at the engagement party.

She replied with a sad-face emoji and apologized for not being able to see him sooner. It was fine. It gave him a moment to look out his hotel window and appreciate being home, although he was a long way from the suburbs he grew up in. In fact, he barely spent much time downtown while he grew up. It was too expensive and claustrophobic for both his and his mother's tastes.

He suddenly felt it, just as the peace of the view was about to overtake him. A pang of recognition hit him, and suddenly his consciousness was flying away to another place and time to fix another fucking mistake.

It was a new rip.

Fucking hell. Never a moment's peace

His mind came to a rest at what looked like a futuristic version of the Chicago he had just left. The sky was a bit rosier despite being midday, but otherwise it looked very similar.

The dusty rose-hued sky suddenly tore itself apart, a paper-shredding sound deafening those that were on the ground going about their lives. These humans were much taller than the ones in his native world, and spoke in a very quick and unintelligible babble, but they still looked human. Crowds of them grabbed their ears to protect against the sound, but no sooner had it ceased, the creature emerged.

Like a Lovecraftian nightmare, a tentacled monstrosity fell through the sky with a roar, appendages flailing about while a myriad of grotesque eyeballs looked in every direction.

It wasn't malicious. The monster was likely just as terrified and confused as the people and other living things it was crushing and terrifying. It didn't know what happened. It was likely just going about its horrible monster life when it fell into this strange place. Now everyone was having a bad time and no one knew why.

Well, one person knew why, and it hurt his heart to watch it.

The chaos of his mistake had grown so far beyond microscopic rips in reality that allowed infinitesimal mold spores to skip over worlds. Now scenes like this, with massive loss of life and no logical reason for it happening, were almost a daily occurrence.

He was only Death, and Death did not control these things. It only mitigated the damage as best it could, so Ethan got to work.

He drifted down to the street level as people ran screaming. In truth, he was already everywhere. The creature had fallen and crushed millions of lifeforms already, from people to dogs, massive trees to blades of grass. Ethan felt this needed a more direct touch, though. Sometimes he needed to wade through the mess he made more directly. Really get in there and *feel* the guilt.

Destruction surrounded him as he strolled nonchalantly through the streets of other-Chicago. These kinds of places were really entertaining for him for about a week when he first started this job. Places so close to his reality but still so clearly different. What evolutionary discrepancy happened to make the people so tall? What chemical variance made the sky dusty rose? Why did the air smell like good bourbon?

Oh, never mind, that last one was the bourbon bar across the street. *Pay attention, dumbass.*

After that initial honeymoon period wore off, he just saw it all as variations on a theme. Now he'd seen galaxies rise and fall in a heartbeat, and had watched worlds like this come and go with shocking regularity. Those rises and falls had been natural, though.

This one was his own creation.

First thing he had to do was fix the hole in the sky before who knew what else fell through. With just a thought, he wove realities with his mind, redirecting the masses of soul-light escaping the innumerable victims around him, and passed them into the rip, allowing them to begin to sew the wound together. In a short time the hole was gone. Only the monster remained.

That was the real hazard of his failure. Rips and tears like this one, which were becoming more frequent and significantly larger, needed to be mended with the light the living emanated when they died. So then, instead of taking their place among the great everything, they just acted like a bandage. Their ascension to their proper place was either stopped or delayed, which upset the balance, which created new holes, which caused more destruction like this. It was a vicious cycle.

The only saving grace was that Ethan was a trained pro at handling vicious cycles.

With the wound mended, he stepped closer to one of the ghastly tentacles flailing around nearby, smashing cars and people with equal measure and destruction. Ethan was simply numb. He had work to do. He waited for it to stop moving and tuned out the sounds of horror all around him.

"Hey," he said calmly to one of the tentacle's eyes, a large, octopus-like orb that seemed to recognize him when he spoke. A perk of being Death was that everyone and everything understood you when you spoke. "I hate to be the one to tell you this, but I'm afraid you don't belong here. Well, no shit, right? But what I mean is something really bad is likely about to happen and nothing can stop it. You seem like a nice monster. I'm sure in your home world you get all the hot blob chicks, and you likely get pretty fuckin' freaking with those tentacles, hentai-style, but you took a stroll down the wrong galactic causeway and ended up here. It's a real fucking drag, I admit.

"So, for what it's worth, I'm sorry. I know this is my fault, and I promise you when this is over I'll take you someplace much nicer, but this is really going to suck between now and then."

The first shots Ethan heard rang out. Some things about Chicago were the same no matter what universe you were in. The creature twitched as some part of it somewhere else started to get shot.

"Yeah, I heard it," Ethan continued, more exhausted than reassuring. "That will be the first step. Bullets aren't likely to do much to you, but what comes after sure as shit will."

The wild creature's eye just looked at him, almost pleading for help. It never asked for this.

"Yeah, I know, it's really fuckin' scary. I can't imagine, man. Or woman? Nah, you don't really deal in gender, do you. That's just my narrow human mind showing through.

"Look, I can't help you, and everything between here and the end is going to blow donkey cock, but I'm working on it. I swear. I don't want this to happen anymore, and this is just a byproduct of something you had no part in. Life isn't fair, my big slimy friend. But I'll stay. I'll be here until the end. I owe you that much."

It was about a half-hour later when the first missile strike hit. In that time, the creature did seem to calm slightly. It wasn't pleased with having some of its eyes shot out, but it stopped its thrashing and rested, in pain but much calmer than when it arrived.

It took three Maverick missiles to finally break through its outer layer and expose the gooey insides. After that it was academic.

Ethan stayed true to his word and didn't leave. When the last missile ripped through its body and exploded, raining down hot liquid grossness all over downtown other-Chicago, the creature didn't even flinch, and Ethan did as he promised and guided the light of the creature to the afterlife with all the love and care his fucked-up and busted heart could muster.

Ethan's mind returned to the body he knew best, still standing in his hotel window looking out over the city of his youth. It wasn't much, and despite what people tried to tell him all his life, the pizza of choice was still highly suspect, but it was home.

He'd seen a ton like the one he had just come from, but they really were getting worse. The ripples created from his loss were getting bigger instead of smaller, and causing ripples of their own in the process. How long before he couldn't keep it together? And what was the endgame? Eternity of fixing his mistake, or the outright death of everything everywhere ever. Why? Why did he deserve this? What possible reason was there for him, of all living things in history, to be the one who had to endure this?

He snapped back, angry at himself for feeling so low again. This wasn't the time. He had a job and he had to do it, but he also had a life he had to participate in as well. It was a small distraction, but a welcome one.

He looked at himself in the shitty hotel bathroom mirror that never showed enough to get a good idea of how one looked, changed outfits with the metaphorical snap of his fingers (one of the benefits of being a deity), decided he was as good as he was going to get, and went out to be cripplingly socially awkward with all of his sister's friends.

Watch out, Chicago. Death was home and was hitting the town.

CHAPTER 5

Ethan opted for a walk the short distance to his destination to mentally wash off the events in the hotel room and arrived at the restaurant his sister instructed fifteen minutes before he was scheduled to show up. Being Death had taught him to be prompt to his meetings, and being early was consistently regarded as being superior to being late.

The place was pretty generic, if he had to put a descriptor to it. Lots of wood. Lights too dark to read by but too light to feel cozy. An open window to the kitchen so the patrons could see a bunch of underpaid staff fight their way through the dinner rush and try to do the best they could with presentation while knowing they were *dangerously* short on arugula.

The seats around the bar were occupied as the Blackhawks played. No one was overdressed since it was a weekend, and most looked like tourists anyway. Who else would go downtown on a Saturday night?

He asked the hostess about where he should go, and she guided him to a separate room in the rear of the place. Inside was a collection of large tables, a private bar, and a handful of people milling around laughing and seemingly having a good time. It was basically Ethan's hell.

Arlene saw him as he entered and broke away from the conversation she was involved in at once, a big smile coming to her face. The red glow of cherry cheeks told him she was already well into it (she had less of his predilection towards sobriety, though a drink could be found in his hand from time to time), but he still welcomed her happiness regardless of how alcohol-fueled it was.

"Hey loser!" she chimed as she hugged him. "You're early! They're still setting up."

"Better early than late, sis. Besides, I wanted to say 'hi' before things got started and I won't be able to get an ounce of your time."

"Oh whatever. Like I said: you're the only family I've got here. You are at the head of my class!"

His eyes rolled with genuine discomfort. "Yippee."

She playfully smacked his shoulder. "Oh whatever. Suck it up, cupcake. You agreed to this. I gave you an out."

"No you didn't. You said I owed you."

She smiled wide once more. "Oh yeah! Well now I'll make sure I milk every last ounce of good will out of you between now and July."

He snorted. Good will? What a laugh.

She pulled him over to her little crowd of friends she had broken away from and made some quick introductions. He had met her fiancé Matthew twice before. Arlene had hooked up with him shortly after Ethan's crash and subsequent job interview. Matthew was fine. No noticeable issues Ethan could see. Handsome enough. Dressed well. Kinda dry. After their shared unpleasant upbringing, finding someone who was a good person and generally inoffensive was likely the best either of the siblings could ever hope for.

"Hey Ethan, thank you so much for coming," Matthew said with what appeared to be actual appreciation and a handshake that didn't seem to be trying to one-up the one Ethan returned. "It means a lot to both of us. Really."

Ethan nodded back. "Hey, my pleasure. For real. Congratulations to both of you." It was the most non-sarcastic or dour he felt he could be at the time. Maybe he *would* end up at the bar before the night was over.

Further introductions to the wedding party followed, who seemed to be the only people in the room upon his arrival. The groomsmen all looked like carbon-copies of Matthew with slight tweaks to height or hair color, and the two bridesmaids there looked like the men's XX chromosome doppelgangers. Arlene really had escaped her youth and was now firmly entrenched in the land of khakis and WASPs, for better or worse.

"There's one more coming but she said she would be a bit late," Arlene informed him. "Vic is not the punctual kind of person, but I'll be sure to introduce you when she gets here. She's small, but she's hard to miss."

Soon the party started in earnest and the room filled up with more practically indistinguishable young professionals, a handful of older folks Ethan assumed were Matthew's parents or family, and a whole lot of honesty, joy and revelry. It was the kind of thing that would make him squirm once upon a time. So many smiles and people without a single care in the world. People who had no idea the things he had seen. The gruesome accidents. The fires. The monstrosities crushing cities and exploding on the populous. Just one world could hold enough horrors to give a person nightmares for a lifetime. Near-infinite worlds? Well, Ethan was just happy he had developed a thick skin. And no matter how many mind-fucking grotesqueries he saw, there likely wasn't much worse than a room full of smiling, happy people.

Ethan did his part, his abrasive nature pushing the limits of his promised eighty percent at times, but whenever things seemed to be a bit dicey he would just excuse himself and head to the bar. By about the fourth or fifth time this happened, the bartender had a fresh cranberry and soda ready and waiting for him. He enjoyed the drink because it looked like booze and tasted like practically nothing.

He stood next to the bar for a bit after quick speeches were made (*don't call me out, don't call me out, don't call me out… damn it, Arlene! Alright, wave to the people, dumbass. Try not to look like a massive tool*) and surveyed the room. A voice in the back of his head told him that with just a quick peek he could likely ascertain a bunch of information about everybody in the room, but decided against it. He didn't want to see something dark about them. Leading with "Hey, heart attacks while shoveling snow are a real bitch, aren't they? Hint, hint…" likely wouldn't fly well here. Even with his job and all the powers it brought with it, Ethan's humanity was key to his success, and his humanity insisted he not invade the cosmos to dig up dirt on his fellow partygoers. He may have been omniscient, and an asshole, but he was also sorta polite.

People came and went so frequently that he never noticed the shadow roll in beside him. "You look at this room with enough uncomfortable animosity that you could film a nature documentary about it," came a female voice he didn't recognize cutting through his haze.

He turned to his right and saw the speaker, a shorter woman with thick-framed glasses and a smooth, wry smile. Despite his promise to his sister, some things couldn't be stopped. He didn't even hesitate. His mouth was a hair-trigger with no guard.

"Yeah, that's the kind of show you make kids watch in sixth grade with Sir David Attenborough talking about how 'the circle of life will eventually claim the young stranger, but for now he's happy to just watch the blossoming fields of yuppies at play. They truly are nature's greatest accident.'"

Fucking. Hell. Ethan.

Her brown eyes went wide behind her glasses. "Damn, man, I didn't mean to offend. Just trying to lighten the mood. You were looking pretty dour with your pink drink over here. Sorry if I hit a nerve."

Ethan waved her off, embarrassed, "No, no, that's just me being me. Sorry. This isn't really my scene. Well duh, that much is obvious. I came as a favor to someone and I'm just trying my best not to drown in awkwardness."

She relaxed at his candor. "Ah, I get it. Sorry. Maybe I shouldn't have come in so hot anyway. This isn't really my crowd either. I mean, I worked with some of them, but I doubt many even remember my name." She extended her hand. "Victoria."

Ethan grasped her hand and returned the pleasantries. "Pleasure,

Victoria. Ethan. Sorry for calling you a yuppie."

"It's fine, I am. Or at least I have been a few times in my life," she replied, releasing his hand. "Your sister warned me you don't have much of a filter."

He looked at her curiously, and then found Arlene. His sister just waved, clearly tanked. Ah, it clicked. Victoria = Vic, the late-coming bridesmaid. He still hadn't been introduced, so it took a moment to come together. Curse his feeble human brain. "I don't, but that's the hazard of being so damned charismatic. I assume I can get away with anything."

Victoria shrugged. "A blessing and a curse, for sure. Can I buy you a drink?"

Ethan's heart was immediately in his throat, anxiety hitting him like a rogue wave crashing on a rocky shoreline. He had just met this woman, and knew nothing about her, and had zero reason whatsoever for thinking the act was anything other than a social kindness, but that all meant absolutely nothing to the chronically and at times fatally disquieted. "I, uh… I'm sorry, I don't really drink."

She flashed her eyes at the glass in his hand and looked back at him, saying nothing. Ethan realized how stupid he looked. The good thing about constantly looking stupid was that eventually you could use it to your advantage. "Oh, don't mind this. This is just a prop I use to make it look like I belong in public."

"Ah-ha," she replied, followed by asking the bartender for another drink for herself, and informing him that if he did want something else that it was on her. "It really meant a lot to Arlene that you came, just so you know. I don't know much about your history, but I can sure as hell tell that there is one, so consider this a way of saying thanks. That is, if you ever actually drink anything."

"Well, if I do have something, I promise you I'll be thinking about how amazing and awesome I am the whole time. After all, I deserve it."

She smiled, grabbed her drink (which looked significantly more masculine than his did) and turned to leave. Ethan thanked Victoria for the gesture, and she went back out into the ever-jubilant crowd.

The rest of the night played out exactly as Ethan predicted, with people enjoying the moment and toasting the happy couple. Ethan was honestly and truly happy for his big sister. A nuclear family deep in the heart of Texas would be icing on the cake for someone like her, if she wanted that kind of thing. He could easily see her swearing and getting rambunctious at PTA meetings, making the traditional southern flowers wilt a little bit with her angry Mid-West sailor mouth. Ethan had no idea if she even wanted kids, or how long they were going to be staying in the Friendship State, but the imaginary scenario still made him smile.

Arlene came over after a while, likely seeing his growing desire to leave. "I relieve you of your duties, sir," she said, half-slurring. "I shall not ask you to mingle with the rabble anymore this night."

He chuckled and tilted what was likely his sixth cran-and-soda. "I don't want to shit in your Cheerios, Arlene. I'm doing just fine."

"Ha, bullshit!" she replied. "You can't lie to me, dick. Go. Honestly, get out of here. You're good, I swear. You've been a good boy. Go enjoy the rest of your night."

"Enjoy what? I'll just go to bed anyway."

"Good, then do that! But meet me for brunch tomorrow, okay? Unless you have plans." He cocked an eyebrow at her. "Ha! I'm funny. Come out tomorrow and eat fucking pancakes with us. My treat."

He snapped his fingers and pointed at her in victory. "Boom, you said it. Your treat. I'm gonna eat so much steak. Steak covered in truffles and gold-leaf. That good Wagyu shit."

"This is Chicago, Ethan. All they can do is take a regular steak and burn the outside."

"That's a deal." He hugged Arlene goodbye, reveling in his minor victory of a forthcoming paid meal, and bid the urban-bourgeois crowd adieu.

CHAPTER 6

Death did not sleep, and Ethan passed the time doing his job until it was time to go the next morning, reaching out through the worlds and passages of the eternal and mending what broken things he could along the way. He felt invigorated by the events of the evening, mostly because he didn't fuck it up. A victory if ever there was one.

Work was always a pain, but after a quick flit to a place he knew that made his favorite coffee to get himself going, as well as a change of clothes so he didn't look like a complete knob and show up in the same thing he wore the night before, he went to meet his sister a brunch place outside of the core of the city and closer to the suburban landscapes he was more familiar with.

It was actually a Mexican place, which he appreciated because he couldn't really stand traditional brunch, and he hadn't had a decent tamale in ages. The sad truth about being everywhere is that he never had time to be anywhere, so although he could magically appear at some taqueria in Sinaloa any time he wanted, he was too unimaginative to actually try when he had a moment to do so.

He entered and saw his sister, as well as Matthew. Not surprising, considering they were engaged and whatever, but also not completely expected as he had just assumed this was a tete-a-tete with Arlene about personal sibling stuff. Whatever. Not the end of the world.

And then Victoria sat at the table just as he was making his way over to it, her hair back in a casual ponytail, and that same Godforsaken anxious flutter that impending social interaction brought with it hit him square in the chest.

It wasn't even that she was drop-dead gorgeous and he was head-over-heels twitterpated or anything like that. Sure she was attractive, but a lot of people were. Whoop-de-do. It was just the mental hurdles he had to now overcome, going from comfort with Arlene, to being peaceful-yet-honest awkwardness with Arlene and Matthew, to now being not a massive cock-nugget with all three of them. There was no hope for it, though. The desire for a nice morning and free meal with his sister had become his undoing.

He made his pleasantries and joined them. Arlene and Matthew looked like hot garbage covered in makeup and aftershave, respectively, but given the party the night before that was to be expected. It was surprising they were even up, honestly. Victoria seemed in a bit better shape, but only barely. The follow-up to the youthful walk-of-shame seemed to be the brunch-of-mild-regret.

"Hey, Cran-And-Soda, good to see you again," she said happily before turning to her menu.

"Hi Ethan," Arlene chimed in. "I hope you don't mind we invited Vic along. She lives pretty far out of town and stayed at a hotel last night, and we thought it'd be rude to ask her to come into town just to party and then leave."

"Thanks, Arlene. Appreciated," she replied without looking up from her menu.

And so the meal continued. It wasn't the worst Mexican he'd ever had, but it sure as hot shit wasn't the best. At one point Matthew ordered mimosas for the table, before looking at Ethan and apologizing. "Sorry Ethan, is that alright? I know you're not much of a drinker, but you're not in AA or recovering from something, are you? I shouldn't have assumed."

Ethan genuinely appreciated the gesture. "Nah man, it's all good. I don't mind. I drink. Not much, but I'm just usually so busy that I never get a chance. Despite our mutual upbringing in the House That Jack and Johnnie built, neither of us is dry, obviously." He motioned to his obviously hungover sister, who flipped him the bird in response. Soon the fizzy beverage symbol of middle-class Sundays was all around the table, only this time with a Mexican chilies and lime juice twist. Ethan didn't hate it at all.

The conversations went from wedding things to home things, to work things, to nothing in particular, all the while Ethan soaked up the moment of normalcy, enjoying the obvious looks of love and affection his sister shared with the decent yet borderline-banal man she had fallen for.

Things got dicey when Matthew asked Ethan about his work. Despite having the song and dance well-rehearsed at this point, Ethan still was cautious to tread lightly and give very little away. "Marketing is marketing, man. People sure love buying shit... er... things, and my company sure loves giving them new ways to do it. I'm all over the place. Last week I was in Canada. Next week I need to go to Spain. Hell, I'll likely be on the moon before too long. It's good to be in demand, but it's tiring."

Matthew nodded his head in mock-understanding. It occurred to Ethan that he didn't have a clue what Matthew did for a living. Or Arlene for that matter. Then the sad truth hit him that he didn't really give a damn, either. It didn't matter. Sooner or later, Death came for them all.

A quick reminder that Ethan was expected to carry his sister's soul away when her time came if he was still in the job. That would just fucking break him...

"So," Matthew continued, "Arlene mentioned something pretty bad happened recently. She said you seemed pretty put out about it when you spoke to her."

Ethan was immediately on the defensive, but relaxed when he saw actual concern in the man's face. This guy had no idea. Not a fucking shred of an idea. How did Ethan explain it, or better yet, change the subject without sounding like a total prick?

"Yeah, yeah there was. I won't bore you with the details, but there was a company... well, honestly it was just one guy... and he was asked to leave peacefully to help my job. He decided to leave in a way that was decidedly not that, and the company is still recovering from it. It did a lot of damage."

The table seemed somewhat enthralled. "Was anyone hurt?" Victoria asked, eyes no longer on the menu.

Ethan could only half-smile. The truth and scope of his fuck-up was so unknowable to them, but the most basic, honest truth was as human and relatable as anything could be, so he went with that.

"Only our pride."

Ethan begged to let that be the end of it. Thankfully his wish was granted, and the conversation turned to more mundane territory. Bullet officially dodged.

A few hours, a few bubbly orange juices, and more than a few mediocre tamales later, Arlene let the table know that they had to go. "Gotta go do some stuff. Home stuff. Work stuff. Boring stuff. Hate to leave you guys."

"Yeah," said Victoria, "I likely need to think about going soon too. I'll keep your brother company until he gets bored of me." Ethan desperately tried not to have his face go flush. He assumed he failed.

Ethan shook Matthew's hand and hugged Arlene goodbye. "Will you be around long? When are you leaving again?" Ethan shrugged, committing to nothing. The conversations they'd shared had let everyone know that his schedule, although busy, was also whatever he made it.

"I'll pop back in again between here and the summer, don't worry. You guys just let me know what you need from me between now and then."

They agreed. "Dress fitting will be next. Maybe in about a month or so? It's girly, but I seriously want you there."

"Good lord, why?"

"Because you won't lie to me if something looks like shit." Fair enough. He couldn't argue with that.

With another hug and a wave, the couple left. Now only the nearly insurmountable wall of social blundering with a stranger remained.

"So, marketing think-tank, eh? How did you ever end up with a job like that?" She was clearly making small talk, but it was better than silence.

There was an unspoken question about how much this woman knew about him as well. Did she know all his history? Did she know about the plane? His miracle survival? Best to assume not until told otherwise.

"Well, I was a bit lost after I left our mom, and kinda directionless for a while. I achieved a bit of local fame for a little bit which put me on the radar of this company and their…" Horrible? Dick-ish? Smart-Mouthed Pile of Shit? "…unique boss. After some thinking and getting my head out of my own ass and realizing what an opportunity it could be, I took the job and here I am. Good pay. Easy schedule. Frequent travel. I honestly lucked out." A lie. Total fabrication. At no point did he actually feel "lucky" to be the ever-creeping specter of death.

"With no education?"

"Nope. Nothing worth speaking of, anyway. High school and hard knocks."

She had him firmly in sight now. "And in spite of this continued air of apathy and general social stumbling?"

Ouch. Deep cut, lady. "Apparently," was all he replied.

"And what was the celebrity event? What put you on that radar?" Ah. She didn't know. She'd find out the moment she googled his name, but for now he was coy. He hated describing what had happened.

"I had a bit of a run-in with mass-transit that seemed to capture people's imaginations for a short time."

She did not look impressed. "That's it? That's the stupidest, most vague answer I could have heard."

"That's all I'm willing to give to someone I just met last night."

"Huh. Okay then." She sat back, flute of fancy OJ in her fingertips. "And your mother? Did you actually leave her, or were you kinda forced out?"

Jeez, now she was just going straight for the jugular, wasn't she. "Oh, now I think you're dancing pretty close to 'too personal for a Sunday brunch meet-cute', Vic."

"Is this a meet-cute?"

Shit, his mouth was leading the way again.

"It's a 'meet', and I know I'm cute, so I just assumed..." Ethan and his inability to shut up: coming soon to a diner near you.

Victoria assessed him. Ethan could feel her brain grinding through what the fuck this guy across from her was actually all about. She didn't seem to want to let the topic die just yet.

"And you actually walked away from her? From your own mother?" It was an honest question rather than accusatory. He appreciated that she was honest. Pulled punches hurt less, but also got less accomplished.

"I walked away from a very bad situation. That situation just had the unfortunate caveat that it *was* my mother. Same-yet-different if you ask me."

Vic nodded in semi-understanding, her ponytail bobbing as it did so. "I gotta say, that's pretty impressive."

Ethan raised an eyebrow. "Impressive isn't what most people would call it. Some may even call it fucking over your own mother and sending her rocketing to her grave for your own selfishness."

There was a softness in her eyes now. "Do you believe that?" Ethan appreciated her forwardness. Not many people dealt with the topic of his mother this well.

He did more than believe it; he actually knew for a fact that it was true. Not that he could tell her that or how he knew. "Let's say I find it very easy to believe."

Silence for a moment before she spoke again. "I can't really say much. My parents are happy and healthy, though getting on in years. I'm not going to sit here and tell you your business." He appreciated that. "But let me tell you, shitty situations look shitty even when you leave them and your vision clears a bit. At least you were honest with me."

"It wasn't me, it was the mimosas. That shit goes straight to my head."

"Well, whatever it was, I appreciate it. It makes this next part a lot easier."

He had no idea what she was referring to. His inability to read people, especially women, transcended space and time. "And what's the next part?"

She leaned back confidently. "The next part is where I ask if you want to go out sometime. I know you're not a local anymore, but if you're sticking around for a bit I'd be happy to..." and then everything else she said just became a complete blur to Ethan.

Did... did she just ask him out? Did this young, professional woman just unintentionally ask *Death* out on a date? The nervous laughter inside Ethan's head fueled by the trifecta of past trauma, current anxiety, and the love of the hilariously absurd grew and grew until it was almost deafening. He didn't even notice that she had stopped talking after a moment. Jesus Christ, he hoped he hadn't been neck-deep in his own head for too long. It didn't look like it, but he felt like he could have been.

There was a moment, brief as it was, where the entity of Death completely evaporated. All that was left was Ethan, for better or worse. Cold. Distant. Defensive to the extreme. This woman was nobody to him, just a friend of Arlene's. So why do this after only meeting him the night before (while intoxicated)? He could only come up with one conclusion. It was an answer that he hated, but had seen an alarming amount of in his time after getting pulled from Puget Sound. Some people had something called "Fixer Syndrome". He had researched the term after he was contacted by so many people, women and men, who wanted to date him or marry him or just get with him after the crash, seeing how hurt and damaged he apparently was. They saw him as a project to be completed rather than an actual human being. He suspected there was more than a little of that in Amy the Admin back in the day. Was that what Victoria was suffering from? The only way to find out anything was to start asking the question.

"Look, I really do appreciate it, but be honest with me: is this your 'thing'? Do you look for lost cats as well? I don't mean to be rude, and I know that there's not really a way I can say this without sounding like it… look, I don't know what Arlene has told you about me, but I'm not some busted emo sad-sack who needs to be fixed or just needs to get laid or anything like that."

The words were out before he could stop them, but that would likely be the epitaph on his gravestone (if he was ever allowed to have one). Death could evoke fear in people, but only Ethan could dive-bomb a human interaction on this kind of scale.

Victoria didn't flinch. She stayed incredibly cool in the face of what this dirt-bag brother of a friend of hers had just accused her of. "Ethan, I can't fix a broken light switch, let alone whatever the hell is going one up there," she hectically motioned to his head with both of her hands as if she was spreading colored paint on a canvas like a toddler, "but I like honesty, I like respectfulness, and I like what you're doing here for your sister even though it *obviously* makes you uncomfortable as hell. And I figured there was a very likely chance that when you leave this quaint faux-Mexican place that I can tell you is in actuality run by a husband and wife from Serbia, that I wouldn't see you again until July. When I realized that thought made me a bit sad, I shot my shot. No subterfuge. And yeah, I don't really know you, but I know Arlene and she still loves you despite some traumatic shit for both of you, but I suspect more for you since you're the younger one. I only kinda know about you mom since she doesn't bring it up, and the word 'dad' hasn't been mentioned once, so that's an easy dot to connect, and anyone with eyes can see what kind of person you are, and I mean that in a complimentary way. You are obviously a straight shooter, so I'm replying in-kind. And frankly I'm getting a bit twitchy, and I would really appreciate it if you would stop me from rambling on…"

Ethan waved his hands, desperate to stop the wave of words pouring from her mouth, each one making him more and more uncomfortable. "Okay, I'll stop you, I'll stop you. Listen, when you've seen the things I've seen, the defensiveness comes naturally. I just have a hard time wrapping my mind around…" He paused, looking at her and her expression of both curiosity and dread. She was confident in her skin, but there was still some timidity there, well hidden. "Fuck it. Sure. If you're being honest with me and you don't see a puzzle missing pieces when you look at me and you feel that you and only you are the one to have those matching pieces, I'll be around. I can stretch it a day or two. It would be nice to know someone at the wedding other than the most important person in the room the whole night."

"What about Matthew?"

"Have you never been to a wedding before? The bride gets gussied up like a princess and every groom wears a variation on the same tuxedo. It's pretty damn clear where the focus needs to be. So sure, I'd like some time out with a friendly face. What's your schedule?"

Victoria shrugged. "Wide open. You free tomorrow?"

"What time?"

"Any time."

He appraised her. "You don't work?"

She shook her head. "I am 'between opportunities', as they say."

She didn't strike him as the kind of person who avoided work, but that was none of his business. At least, not yet. "Ok, I'm game. Lunch somewhere? Should we meet? Where do you live?"

He could see her face get a bit sheepish. "Uh, yeah, about that… Valparaiso." She almost flinched saying it.

Ethan laughed. "Valpo? Yea, no wonder you didn't go home last night. What a shit-show that would have been. So then what's your plan here?"

A flash of relief in her eyes. "I didn't honestly have one. I just asked and figured we could work out the details later. I can come back into the city if you'd like. I wasn't lying when your sister and Matthew left, though. I do need to get home today."

"No, no need to make this any more awkward for you. I can come

to you. Honestly. It's not a big deal. Where and when?"

She relaxed. This really seemed to be a test for her. "Are you sure? It's all the way out there. We could meet halfway or something?"

"I am *not* meeting in Hammond... Do you know how much the crime rate jumps between Valpo and there? It's like a crypto price ticker. Up, down, up, down, and they are decidedly 'up'. Nah, It's fine. Valpo it is. Gets me out of the city. Well, sorta. Out enough."

She retreated. The battle of "who can be nicer" was firmly his. "See, I was right," she pulled out her phone, "you're not the ass you pretend to be."

"I really am. But I'm trying to reform. It's harder than smoking to quit cold turkey." She gestured to his phone laying face-down on the table and he handed it over. A tap and an invisible exchange of information later and Victoria and Ethan were linked by the only bond worth a damn to the younger generation in the early twenty-first century.

"There's a nice Italian place on Calumet Avenue, if that's alright. I'll send you the address. Thanks again for coming out there even though I'm the one who asked. Must be nice to have such a flexible schedule. Maybe I'm in the wrong industry."

"I thought you weren't in any industry at the moment?"

She placed her phone in her clutch and hesitated. He had just hit a nerve and he didn't even realize it. Fucking social interactions and their traps! "You know what I mean. When I am employed, 'marketing think-tank' seems to pay a lot better than the title suggests."

"It has its good days and bad." Mostly bad. Pretty much all bad these days. "I'll be there. Noon?"

She shook her head. "Is one alright?"

"One is fine. If I'm going to drive an hour, I don't mind the extra sleep first."

"If you can get from here to there in an hour then you're a more aggressive driver than you look." She stood. Like some debonaire Victorian dipshit meeting the Queen of Versailles, Ethan stood as well. Where the hell had he gotten manners from? It sure wasn't from the woman who once screamed at him, "If you want toilet paper, then what the fuck is the laundry machine for?! Use a sock!"

"One o'clock. Italian. Valpo. Lunch with Vicky."

She stopped dead, looked him in his eyes with enough force to stop a bullet, and spoke very clearly. "I just met you, so you get one free pass. Call me that again and I will castrate you on The Bean on a sunny day and have it cook your manhood while you watch. And I mean that in the politest of ways. Victoria, Vic, or V. 'Vicky' will get you killed."

Now that was an attitude he could stand against with ease. "All I heard in that threat was you're thinking about getting your hands on my hot manhood."

A serious face met him. *Shit. Shit shit shit. Why the fuck would you say that, you pile of insecure entrails in human form!*

Being Death the previous two years had certainly increased his confidence, but whittled away whatever filter he may have once had.

Victoria eventually cracked, bursting out into a pure, clean laugh. The mood lightened like a million tons was raised from the roof of the world. "You got me there, Mr. Dessier. You have got me there." She outstretched her hand and he took it, fighting his eyes not to look downwards, forcing them to hold hers, not out of intimidation but out of actual courtesy. "I'll see you tomorrow."

With a quick nod and a shuffle out from between the table and chair, she was gone.

Ethan stood at the table, and then crashed back into the chair, drawing curious looks from all around him. What the fuck did he just do?

Judging by the wink and thumbs-up the old man at the table next to him flashed when he looked around, Ethan thought it may not have been something extremely stupid for once.

CHAPTER 7

The I90 turnoff towards Hammond, Indiana was mostly empty, the rush of the morning now gone and the midday sun hanging high in the chilly air.

He sat there, pulled off to the side, his cheap and generally unloved car idling noisily as vehicles whizzed past. Some gave him a curious look. Others ignored him. More than one gave him the finger for no good reason other than it was an action that had very little consequences while driving by at fifty-five miles per hour.

He didn't care, though. He made it as far as his increasingly hazy brain would let him, thankful that he didn't hit anyone along the way. It was a risk when he set out, but he refused to be at home when it happened. He couldn't let his wife find him. It was better to do this to a stranger. It made him feel less guilty.

To his dismay, a car slowed down and pulled over in front of him. It was black and new, and looked very clean despite the state of the highways around here. *Damn it. Don't get involved! Just keep driving! Assume I'm having car trouble or something. Please God, do not...*

A man got out of the car.

Shit!

A young man dressed head to toe in black approached the window and gave the universal-yet-outdated hand gesture for "please roll this down". No. No way. The haze was growing thicker now and it wouldn't be much longer.

The man made the motion again, mouthing the word "please?".

Oh fine. Maybe he could just lie to him and make him clear the fuck off. He pressed the button, and with a bit of difficulty the window rolled down. He got ahead of it right away. "Hey man, it's ok. Really. Just engine trouble. AAA is on the way."

The young man removed his black sunglasses, a look of understanding in his eyes. "Yeah, I'm sure they are. Pretty sure AAA can't fix the problems you're having though, boss."

Confusion from the words as well as the encroaching loss of consciousness. "What do you mean? They just need to tow me or something. It's fine, you can carry on. Thanks for stopping."

The man placed his hands on the door, leaning in. "That'd be a pretty shitty thing to do, letting a poor innocent tow truck driver find you, wouldn't it? That is, if one was coming, which we both know they're not."

This conversation was taking a turn he didn't like. Damn it, he wanted to be alone. He deserved to be alone! Time to cut it off quickly. Maybe he'll get the message then. "I'm fine. You can take off now." He pushed the button for the window to go up and the man pulled his fingers away and raised his hands defensively.

However, instead of leaving, he proceeded to walk around the car and approached the passenger door. Obviously the door was locked, so he had no idea what the guy was trying to accomplish with...

The door popped open easily. He knew it was locked. Knew it! So how the hell did this guy open it?

"Hey," he slurred slightly. Shit, it was really kicking in now. "What the hell are you doing?"

The young man in black casually slipped into the passenger seat while tucking his folded sunglasses into a coat pocket. "I'm getting into your car, obviously. Jeez, calm the fuck down."

After closing the door again, the man just sat there, passively looking at him like a puppy behind glass that he was thinking about buying.

"Get... get the hell out of... of my car." Things were getting blurry.

"No. No I will not, David. Can I call you Dave? Fuck it, I'm going to call you Dave anyway. No. I'm going to sit right here."

"Wha…? How the fuck do you know my name?"

The man waved his question off like a fly was stuck in the car. "Oh whatever, man. That's the least of your worries right now, David Richard Connelly. The point is I'm here, and I'm not going to leave. Not until this is over."

How did this guy know his name? His *full* name? He never used "Richard" on anything. He hated having Dick for a name.

That wasn't important now. He instead attempted to push the man out, even though the door was closed. His brain clearly wasn't functioning at 100% anymore, and the attempt was laughable.

"Ha, really?" the young man laughed. "You're going to try and force me out? Jesus David Dick, you drank enough vodka and dropped enough Oxy to castrate a water buffalo about ten minutes ago and you think you stand any chance against me in the state you're in right now? You're delusional."

He was right. Dave's arms felt like wet noodles by this point, and the man in black beside him was starting to float through his vision. "What… what do you want?"

The man nodded. "A reasonable question. I want to be here when you die, Dave. Usually it's my professional responsibility to do so, but seeing as you were right here, right now, while I was on my way to something important, I considered it a sign that I should take a personal interest in your situation. This is human me and inhuman me meeting to achieve the same ends."

"Why? What's it to you if I die?"

"Oh there's no 'if' involved anymore, Dave. It's as sure as the sun and stars."

Something about the way he said that scared the shit out of David Connelly. What function he had left in his brain made him think he may have made a mistake. "Why does it matter to you? Who the fuck am I to you?"

"Nobody, Dave. Not a single body. But you're a human. I'm a human, or at least I used to be, and that's enough. I've seen enough death to know someone should not die alone if they can avoid it. Even if they think it's for the best."

Dave's head tilted as he tried to focus on the young man. "It is. It is for the best."

"No, it's not. In fact, it would have been better if you didn't do this at all. It's a big-ass world out there, Dave. You owed it to yourself and everyone who ever loved you to scour every inch of it for help before taking this step. But here we fucking are, right? Jeez, suicide is just the fucking worst."

"Why? No one… no one cares." He was having trouble keeping his eyes open now, and it felt like a truck was slowly being lowered onto his chest.

"I won't even start listing the people who care about you, man, but they are out there. I promise you. Even me, some guy off the street, genuinely cares about you. Human beings are empathetic. At least the decent ones are. We don't like seeing others in pain. And you are in pain, and we want to help you. Well, 'wanted' to help you, anyway. Not much we can do now. I mean, I'll do what I can from here on out, but that sleepy ship is sailing and there is no going back to port."

It wasn't true. It couldn't be. Dave had his problems and just about everyone abandoned him instead of helping him. His kids stopped calling. His wife was almost certainly having an affair. He had to leave like this just to stop bringing others down.

"Oh yeah, I see that look in your eyes," the man said coolly. "That 'this is the best way, everyone left me, I deserve this' look. I wish, I *wish* I could tell you how many times I've fucking seen it, and I can tell you that I can count on exactly zero fingers how many times it's actually been true. Now, the professional side of me says that this is just another day at the office, but me, the human side of this coin… my heart is literally breaking for you, Dave. It honestly is. In another life, at another time, if I happened upon you like this, I would have torn the entire Mid-West apart trying to help you.

"But I can't. The other side of me knows that all the efforts in the world won't do anything. That clock of yours is almost done ticking.

It really, really sucks that I know that, but I do. It's a double-edged sword. One side of me knew you were dying here in semi-industrial hell and the human part of me insisted I stop despite how lost the situation was. Hazard of the job."

"What... what job?" His breathing was getting very shallow now.

The man smiled with his mouth, but not his eyes. "Boat captain, dumbass."

"Why... why stay with me?"

The young man rolled his eyes. Possibly his favorite physical action. "Like I said, I want to. The planets aligned to have you here, in this world, at this time, choose this moment to off yourself in a rusted-out Mazda on the side of the I90 at the exact moment I was coming by. Now, I don't believe in fate. Like, at all. But I do still think that somewhere deep inside what is left of me are the remnants of a decent person, and that's the part of me that knew it was a good idea to join you in this car right now."

"Wh... Why?"

"Jeez, you ask that a lot, don't you. Because despite not knowing you from Adam, I actually give a fuck about you and how you die."

The mental cloud was darker than ever now. It was close. David was scared. No, David was fucking terrified.

"I... I don't want to die, man." The words were practically choked out.

"Let me tell you, very few people do when they reach this point. You're not alone there. Just about everyone who goes out like this has that moment of clarity." It was heartbreaking, but he understood it was inevitable. People do what they feel they must do, and those kinds of choices usually come with huge regrets.

There was very little left of his vision and breathing now. It felt as if he was deep under water, the pressure trying to crush his lungs.

"Who... who are you?"

As the lights went out in his eyes and he felt that he couldn't take another breath even if he wanted to, Dave felt a warm, comforting hand slip into his and squeeze gently. He squeezed back, not in desperation anymore since he knew this was officially a one-way trip, but in thanks. The young man was right: he didn't want to die alone.

"My name is Ethan," his voice said, as if David was in a large cave and the sound came echoing from all around him. "And I promise you I won't let you do this on your own."

As he pulled off the interstate and started heading towards beautiful downtown Valparaiso, Indiana, Ethan was in a haze of his own, though not one nearly as bad as poor Dave Connelly had been at the end. This was more of a self-induced fog than a chemical one. Suicides always fucked him up, but he rarely took such a hands-on approach (literally) as he just did with Dave. It really was a cosmic coincidence that he was right there at that moment, just when Ethan had decided to make the drive instead of just blipping himself to the restaurant door.

Ethan hated coincidences with a passion. They were too much like "fate", and his feelings on that concept were abundantly clear.

But still, there he was, on the side of the road holding a stranger's hand as he passed away. Ethan even made sure to call the authorities to let them know. He hated the idea of Dave being found by someone who didn't consider "possible dead body discovery" to be a part of their job description, even if it wasn't ideal. At least paramedics knew the score when they approached a car like Dave's shitty old Mazda. He left the scene moments before the ambulance arrived, lost in thought for the rest of the drive.

Another job well done.

Get your head in the game, stupid, he chided himself. *It's time to step up to the fucking plate and have a human conversation or whatever.*

God, what was he doing here? He had just watched a grown man die. Hell, at this moment he was actually a part of literally trillions of lives being snuffed out, over and over again with every passing second, but so long as he held himself in his regular 'ol Ethan body, that fact seemed like a whisper instead of a roar. He could deal with that. He had trained himself well, young Jedi.

He pulled the car into the parking lot, having ditched the imitation of his mom's old ride like what he had in Canada and instead deciding to go with something ever so slightly more ostentatious in the form of a new Acura. Sure, he could go full-on Ferrari if he wanted to, but he wanted something that was more reasonable. Showing off, without showing up. He knew better than anyone how much the sight of money can make someone uncomfortable.

It didn't matter anyway. Technically the car wasn't even real. Pulling things in and out of the fabric of reality was actually the first trick Ethan learned in this role. It made the job so much easier, particularly when he spent so much time as a living human. Like playing *Grand Theft Auto* with the cheat codes active.

It was only his money he didn't mess with. He earned that settlement money damn it, and he'd be damned if he didn't use it. You can't just go dropping planes on people!

Well, technically the previous Death had manipulated things with a delicate touch in order to make that happen, but he wasn't around to pay up anymore, so this was Ethan's compromise.

Ethan walked in and looked around. The lunch rush had apparently moved on and the place was quiet. Victoria was at the back in a booth in a quiet corner.

God damn, she looked great.

Ethan didn't have a "type". He was never picky about the kind of women he chose to crush on, but Vic was making it easy. Maybe it was the way the sun streamed through the blinds and created the perfect light, or that she looked confident despite not really needing a reason to since she was just looking down at her phone, or maybe it was just nice to see a familiar, friendly face after what had just happened on the way there, but the smile that came to his face when he approached and started to sit down was genuine.

Ethan hated smiling. It gave too much away. Still, he just couldn't help it right now.

As she looked up from her phone and their eyes met, his heart stopped when he realized that she was not smiling in return. She didn't even say hello. Her eyes narrowed, almost as if she was trying to read his face like an optometry patient asked to read the very smallest line of letters on the paper in the distance. Then she looked back at her phone.

"And I quote," she began. He had no clue where this was going and he was suddenly very, very scared. "'The young man many believe to be the lone survivor, one Ethan Dessier of Seattle, Washington, was returning from his mother's funeral at the time of the accident. Our hearts go out to this young man, and we would like him to know that we are all deeply supportive of his recovery, and hope to find others that share his fate in the days to come. So says Mr. Ronald Cramer, President and CEO of the airline.' Ho. Ly. Shit."

Ethan's eyes fell and his shoulders slumped immediately. That hadn't taken long at all. "To be fair, no one gave them permission to print my name when that came out. There's no justice in rogue journalism these days. Did you know that idiot revealing personal information about me likely added a load more money onto the payout they had to give me?"

Her eyes went wide. "So it's true? You're him? The lone survivor of the Puget Plummet?"

"Plunge," he corrected, "Puget Plunge, and I would be a lot happier if that little reveal could have waited until a theoretical second date."

She put the phone down. "I agree, but I got bored since you were a few minutes late. I heard you have no social media presence, and you mentioned being a bit of a celebrity for unknown reasons, so I had to rely on Google. You can't blame me, honestly. A guy your age with no Snap or Twitter is suspicious as hell."

"I have a Reddit account."

Her eyes narrowed once more. "Well now you're even more suspicious."

He tried to deflect. "I'm sorry for being a little late. It's been a while since I've driven this way, and I got a bit," *I won't let you do this on your own*, "tied up on the way. It's been a morning."

"I'm sure it has," she answered, "but did you just try and redirect the conversation away from being the only survivor of the worst aviation disaster the state of Washington had ever seen?"

"Actually the entire Western United States, and the numbers aren't even close. Number one with a bullet."

"I hate to be a bitch about it, but I'm not really joking, Ethan. This is some heavy shit I just found out about my lunch date moments before he sat down."

He'd been through this before. His flippant attitude towards what happened that day was not uncommon. "I'm sorry. Not that I didn't tell you, because you'll forgive me if reliving that is a touchy subject for me, but about being an ass about it. That was a dark period of my life and treating it like I only dropped my DQ Dilly Bar on the sidewalk makes swallowing that pill over and over much easier."

Her face went red. "Oh. Oh my. Ah shit, I'm really sorry. I just thought you were being too dismissive about all those other people. I never... well, it was just so many people. I remember that story so well since it was a plane from Chicago. I was terrified I knew someone on that flight."

"Well, you do now I guess."

She ignored him. That was likely for the best. "Just, all those people. What was it? Eighty-something? Ninety?"

"One hundred and thirteen, present company excluded."

She suddenly looked white, embarrassment flush long-gone. "I'm sorry. I've just never met anyone who has faced that amount of death before."

Ha! Ha ha ha ha ha. Hold it together, Ethan. Laughing right now would be the worst mistake you ever made.

"It's okay. Well, sorta. As much as it can be. Arlene was a big help, and so was finding this job soon after, once I got my head on a bit straighter. I spoke to some doctors of both the body and mind variety and it all seemed to help a bunch." That was actually true. Ethan had scoured the multiverses and found a litany of professionals to speak with. It's amazing what a little mental housecleaning could do, especially in the best hands reality had to offer.

Victoria leaned back in the booth chair and exhaled forcefully, boarding on a whistle. "Phew. Wow. Uh, yeah, so that was a hell of a start, wasn't it."

Not sure if it was a question but eager to lighten the mood, Ethan took the ball and ran with it. "I've had worse. I once went out with someone who brought their mother with them as chaperone."

"That's not that weird."

"It is when the mom had been dead for two years and it was an urn with her picture on it."

Vic looked taken aback for a moment, and then relaxed. A small laugh even came out. She seemed to realize right then and there that this was simply how Ethan Dessier operated, for better or worse. "It's all about death with you today, isn't it."

Ethan shrugged. "It's a topic that's been known to follow me around."

CHAPTER 8

It had been a long time since Ethan had anything even close to resembling a date. Amy had been almost two years ago. He had once considered dabbling in some of the other worlds he could inhabit in an effort to look for love, but the opportunity never arose, and he was pretty confident it was a terrible idea anyway. Work was too much for him at the best of times, and basically impossible to deal with after *that* thing happened. However, Arlene and her upcoming wedding were worth the effort, and as the afternoon went on he realized that there was a large part of him that wanted more human interactions. Strangely enough, Ethan seemed to miss them, a fact that surprised him.

Victoria was much more relaxed now that the heavy and surprising subject of the plane crash was mostly behind them. He could see that every once in a while, there was a spark in her eye and he recognized it as her thinking of something to ask, realizing it may hit a nerve, and then thinking better of it.

Instead, the conversation turned to less painfully personal things. Ethan learned that Vic and Arlene used to work together, but that Vic had to leave for reasons she didn't disclose and he had no right to ask about. She and Arlene had remained friends, but Vic had grown apart from the other girls in the bridal party for one reason or another, but she looked forward to spending time with them all the same. She lived out here now, in the satellite cities of Indiana, helping her parents out until she was ready to jump back into the professional pool. She went to Purdue (*Oh, la de dah. Way to punch above your weight class, champ!*), loved anything peanut butter-related, enjoyed road trips with no destination, and she declared very early on that she could kick his or anyone else's ass at shuffleboard, which she had picked up while visiting and traveling with her grandparents before they had each passed away.

Don't say it, Ethan. Don't say it. Don't say it...

"That's a bold claim, but I'm pretty good at handling tang myself."

Thank you and goodnight, ladies and gentlemen. The doctor of cool has left the building. I will see myself out. Please tip your waitstaff.

Victoria just laughed. If it was genuine, awkward, or just pity (likely pity), he couldn't tell. The gesture was whole-heartedly accepted.

When the subject came around to himself, Ethan did his best not to delve into the negative too much. However, that didn't leave a lot left to mine, truth be told. He talked about how he liked to travel now that he was able to, how he was looking forward to the wedding because Arlene was great and deserved amazing things, how his job was demanding but he enjoyed staying busy, and how he came to love Seattle and its gloomy winters, but a small part of him kinda missed Chicago snow that was heavy enough to make grown men question themselves when they shoveled.

The food was amazing, just as she said it would be, and he was careful not to order something likely to cause a mess like spaghetti or linguini, and the drinks were helping both of them relax even though it was mid-afternoon on a January Monday.

Two days in a row, Ethan thought. *I'm basically a lush at this point.*

However, the most important thing he noticed the whole time was that even though he was "working" all through the cosmos at all times, Ethan and Victoria were having a great time, and that was all he could think about.

That was, until the job, and the hazards of it, could no longer be ignored.

Lunch was just about over when Vic made a new proposal. It

would have been a sweet moment if Ethan hadn't just filled his mouth with what could only be called an irresponsible amount of tiramisu.

"If you're not in a rush, I know a place nearby where we can still hang out and relax if you'd like? I know you came way out here and I'd hate to make you rush off. It's chilly, but still a beautiful day."

Ethan almost choked, the powdered cocoa from the dessert coating his lips as he quickly exhaled. He forgot that regular people followed schedules, and he hadn't been clear on when he needed to leave and go back to Seattle. Naturally, Victoria had assumed it would be soon. It was a small note that the role of Death had messed with Ethan's head in subtle ways.

"Sorry… sorry," he said, his face turning red. It took him a moment to swallow the creamy treat and get himself composed. He had also convinced himself by this point, with a series of bad jokes (*fucking tang?! You moron!*), aloof responses, and his general appearance of malaise (admittedly a birth defect or something of that sort) that by the time this meal was over she would be happy to cast him off and not see him again until their mutual wedding duties aligned and they were forced into the same room together once more.

Once he was convinced he was no longer going to choke on ladyfingers, he composed himself as much as he could and replied. "I'm not in a rush. Where did you have in mind?"

She smiled, apparently happy with the answer. "There's a park with a lake nearby. It's so nice when it's frozen. Kids skating and all that other urban bliss you likely hate. You don't strike me as a 'sit and feed the ducks' kinda guy, but it's a nice day, and I'm sure there's something worth looking at over there."

"Actually, ducks are really amazing animals. I just get really pissed off when I see people feeding them bread. Don't ever do that, by the way. It really fucks with their entire digestive system. I mean, why did anyone ever think that was a good idea? What about game fowl made people think feeding them wheat, milk, yeast, and egg products was natural? I swear to God it's the most…" Victoria had turned red and looked away while he ranted about ducks. *Sunovabitch, what the hell did I do now?* "… Hey, I'm sorry, did I say something stupid? My mouth isn't well supervised at the best of times, and now that I had a drink, like, an hour ago, it's basically a free-for-all in there."

She looked back at him. "No, no it's fine. I like a person who has conviction. It's just that, feeding ducks in the summer is one of my favorite ways to relax."

God-fucking-damn it!

It was Ethan's turn to change color. "No, I'm sorry. You can feed them all you like." Stumble stumble, Ethan. He was talentless at this kind of thing. "Nobody knows better than me the necessity of a good, relaxing moment, and here I just shit on yours like… like…" *Find a simile! Find it! Make it cute! Don't say the one you were just thinking of!*

"Like a duck that just ate a load of Wonder Bread?" she replied.

Ah, perfect, and he wasn't the one who said it. "Yeah, something like that. So, is this place in walking distance, or…?"

"Well, sorta. It's a walk, but it's a nice walk. Or at least, as nice as this town has to offer. Did you drive?" He nodded. Looks like it was time to test the "Fancy-but-not-ostentatious" theory of the Acura, the only brand he could think of that was practical and fancy at the same time. "And you're good to drive?"

He nodded. Drinking was a rarity for him, and getting drunk was basically unheard of. Besides, a perk of the job was the control of such dalliances and control of his physical system. He was fine. "Great!" she said. "Then let's go for a ride. Once we settle the bill, anyway."

"I already looked after it," he said.

"When?"

He shrugged. "When you went off to 'powder your nose' last time. Hope you don't mind."

Her face softened. "No, not at all. Thank you. I just don't want you to take me for a gold-digger with no job trying to land the eligible bachelor. I like to handle my own business when I can."

"Fair enough, I respect that for sure," Ethan replied. *Idiot! This isn't the fucking fifties!* He hadn't meant to be flashy or hyper-masculine or anything like that. He had just thought he should, foolishly. Another hazard of being a generally broken man (although trying hard to get stronger) was that you just assumed responsibility for this kind of thing. "The next one is on you then."

She stood and smiled. "You assume there will be a next one?"

He stood and joined her. He enjoyed the playful banter, but he was also a realist, so he said what was in his heart, the filter from there to his mouth once again taking the direct route instead of passing through the brain-filter. "I think so. We're both having a good time, right? I expect we'll go to the park, then part ways, and see each other again soon. Sooner than the wedding. Maybe even sooner than the dress fitting."

She came close to him. Very close. God damn, he hadn't smelled a woman in so long. His heart fluttered heavily, but honesty was his best policy. "And why do you think that?"

"Because I want to. No, you know what, it's only been a few days, but I need to. Not in a creepy way, I swear, but because in the three days we'd known each other, I think we have a lot to share, and we haven't had enough time to do it."

She stayed close. Did she know how disorientated this made him? Almost certainly. "Fair enough. I don't disagree. Well, let's just go to the park, enjoy each other's company for a bit, and see how accurate you are."

"Sounds good."

Ethan led her out to the car (*A Blacura? I'm going to think of it as a Blacura*) and unlocked the doors. She looked at the car with interest, but said nothing. In retrospect, that was probably the best possible reaction she could have had. Nice enough for attention, not nice enough to comment on. Perfect.

The first pangs of something being wrong hit when they left the parking lot and turned in the direction she had given him. Just as the car straightened out down the road, something popped into his head, almost like a text message from the universe. Another catastrophic event was brewing. Somewhere a rip was about to happen, and a monstrous tentacle creature in a major city may just be the start of it.

He did his best to stay cool as he drove and not show that anything was wrong, but when it happened again as they got closer and the lake came into view, he couldn't hide it anymore. Why the hell had he agreed to keep this afternoon going? Limiting the amount of time he spent as a human should have been the play here.

He looked at his passenger.

Oh. Right. *That's* why.

Victoria noticed this time. "Hey, are you ok? Too much tiramisu?"

"Ha, you can never have enough tiramisu. That shit is like ambrosia. No, just a sudden headache. It happens from time to time." Wow. That was a recovery and a half! She'd just assume it was a holdover from the accident and say nothing more, and maybe he'd score an extra sympathy point or two.

Amazing deflection aside, he still needed to see what was going on. Not all interplanetary disasters caused by the ruptures in space-time (*Jesus, I have a weird job*) needed his direct attention, but sometimes they did. He held his breath as he pulled into the parking lot near the lake and started to step out.

He quickly manifested a bottle of Advil and a thing of water when Vic wasn't looking, feigning taking them from a bag in the back seat. "Forgive me for a moment." She swept her hand in front of herself in a "go ahead" motion. Perfect. That should buy him enough time.

Fighting to hold at least an image of himself in the parking lot, his full consciousness reached out and found the issue.

Shit, he thought. *Double shit.*

His mind awoke in a sea of blue, like he had transported into the heart of a massive crystal with white light bouncing all around him. He didn't know this place at all. He couldn't even sense any kind of life here. It was devoid of anything but ever-changing crystalline fractals growing and shrinking all around him. It was beautiful, but he couldn't see what the issue was. This was a world that had nothing to die.

And then he realized what the problem was. He hoped his

real/fake body back in Indiana didn't just turn white or pass out from fear. And yes, Death could absolutely be afraid. That was something he had learned very early on.

This was not going to be a quick and easy fix. Although gigantic and horrible, with ongoing repercussions that were still going on, the event in other-Chicago two days ago was relatively clean. This was about to get manure-pile dirty.

He quickly went back to his body, which had just finished drinking the water after taking two (fake) pills. He still had very little taste for painkillers of any kind. Dave and his Oxy from earlier had emphasized that even more.

He had to think quickly. Not his strong suit. Fuck, why right now?

No. No, he could do this. Death was allowed to have a life. He just needed to think, and soon enough he had an idea.

He started to walk around the front of the car and join Victoria when his phone started vibrating in his pocket.

"Oh jeez," he said, pulling it out. "I'm really sorry. I should have turned this off."

Victoria waved him off. "No way, not at all. I'm the one that asked you out on a weekday. Take it if you need to."

He looked at the screen. For some reason, his fake phone call manifestation had been to have his "boss" call him. When he looked at the phone, the smiling, sun-bleached-blonde image of "Azreal Pana" looked up at him, that idiotic grin mocking Ethan, as if it knew what kind of torture he was going through and he was loving every minute of it.

Even in death, he was an asshole.

"I, uh, I'm sorry, I do need to take this. It shouldn't be long," he explained to her.

"For sure. I'll just be over there," she indicated a snowy bench that looked over the frozen water. "Take your time." She walked off.

Perfect. Another successful lie. The best kind.

Whatever, feel guilty about it later. Let's see what we can do about this fucking problem. He put the phone to his ear and mocked talking.

It was business time.

His mind went back to the crystal world, just in time to see millions of microscopic rips open up, suddenly flooding the white-and-blue space with tiny green specs.

Algae. Millions and millions of tiny specs of algae. He had no idea where they were coming from, but the effect was instantaneous.

When life flooded a place where life could not be sustained, it was usually snuffed out in an instant. That was the case here. As soon as the small green blooms entered this strange universe that they had no place being in, they died rapidly. Death had to take each of those lives and get them where they belonged.

But death was still going on elsewhere, and this sudden, unplanned amount of life invading a dead space effectively added a mountain of unexpected work for Death to deal with. And to his dismay, he could feel more rips opening all the time. Bit by bit this world was being invaded by a bunch of holes too small to see with the naked eye, but the algae blooms were clear as day.

It almost hurt, like each new death of the tiny little plants was a needle under his skin. Unplanned death was the worst kind. Death that he didn't see coming was possible, but rare.

In his "interview" with the previous Death, he had burned down a not-so-small chunk of grassland to make a point. Those deaths had been unplanned, and Death was furious with him about it. His face and reaction seemed to indicate that it wasn't something that had happened before to him, and in his scans of the experiences of previous Deaths, he couldn't find much that said it happened to them, either.

Great, a new twist on the job, just for me.

Whatever. Other problems for other times. He had to fix this.

He did his best to ignore the mental jabs each death caused in him, as well as the beauty of the world around him, like he was inside a living snowflake, which he could have been since life could be massive and miniscule at the same time. Something to investigate later.

As opposed to fixing each new hole bit by bit, he instead used some of the dying plant's essence to create a wave of healing power, passing them over the ruptures like a Japanese hand fan. It succeeded in getting a lot of them, but he couldn't keep up anymore.

Damn it, he needed a new plan. And he had to make it fast because he had a lady waiting on the other side of this job.

Fuck it. Time to go for broke. This was going to get worse instead of better, so after a quick reach into the Everything to see if his new plan would work, he chose a new tact. It was going to hurt in the long run for sure, but there was nothing he could do anymore. The holes kept coming and he had to prevent this death, even at the cost of something beautiful.

He expanded his mind and found the source of the beautiful world he was contained in. It was actually the core of an oxygen atom, randomly floating in space, far from anything. Flotsam of a forming universe.

Good. No witnesses. Can't have the Space Police knocking on my door.

Of course, there were no Space Police. If there were, they would have stopped him a long time ago. He deserved it.

He used more of that life light and expanded them, using his cosmic powers to stretch them over the atom as it drifted. And then, in a trick he'd learned along the way, he used the light of life to constrict quickly, essentially crushing the atom from existence.

The atom imploded, rupturing and blasting outwards in what was surely a sight to see, had anyone been anywhere near it to witness it. The silent explosion in the vastness of space pressed back against the tiny rips within, sealing them in a blink. The algae, which would have been massive compared to the atom if these worlds had been meant to be together but instead was another example of two things that were never meant to meet, suddenly clashed. And all at once something small, innocent, and infinitely beautiful was snuffed from existence. It wasn't alive, but Ethan still felt its loss on a human level.

"Another win for the good guy," he said into the void, his voice shallow and without echo. "It really is amazing that I'm allowed to have this much fun all day."

No time for a pity party, though. Someone was still waiting for him.

He pulled himself back to his "home" body, briefly listening to the crap he was saying to the imaginary Azreal on the other end. Mostly bullshit execu-speak sprinkled with the occasional saucy word. "Azreal" would have appreciated it.

He walked over the crushed paths of snow and joined Vic once more. Her attention was drawn to a clear patch of ice not far from where she was standing.

"Everything okay?" she asked as he approached.

He brushed it off. "Fine, fine. But I could ask you the same thing. What are you looking at?"

She pointed to the ice. "It was weird. See that patch of ice down there?" He nodded. "Well, I was looking at it because the colors underneath it looked amazing since the ice was so clear. A brilliant green, likely from plants or whatever. And then the green just started to vanish, like it was being vacuumed away.

Ethan was sure he went a bit white. What were the odds the algae that was just the cause of the destruction of a harmless atom was from his own world and was so close to where he was at that moment? Mathematically and practically impossible in every way his ever-expanded brain could imagine. Something wasn't right.

"Whatever," she continued, bringing him back from his confused and worried state. "I'm sure it's just some weird event with some kind of scientific explanation I have no idea about because I'm not a science major. Engineering is more my thing. It actually looked kinda cool!"

Yeah, death and destruction often did.

He indicated they go for the proposed walk along the path that followed the shoreline. It was brisk, but the sun was still out and the wind had died away. A nice afternoon for a walk with a pretty lady.

"So other than the duck thing in the summer, do you come here often?"

She reached into her pocket and produced a bag of what looked to be shelled peanuts. "Well, that's a summer thing. In the winter I like to feed the squirrels. Care to join me?"

The joy of sharing a nice moment with Victoria was overshadowed by a simple truth, and even though he agreed and they headed off down the path into the wooded area nearby, Ethan was sure that this was all a joke now.

For reasons he would likely never tell this woman, he fucking hated squirrels.

CHAPTER 9

Ethan had spent most of his life being as emotionally unavailable as possible; not on purpose, but just as a result of a million things that worked against him as he grew up.

So it was a conflict he'd never really experienced before when their afternoon was done and Victoria said she had to go home (which he was happy to take her to), and as she was getting out of the car she hit him with more emotional honesty than he'd ever known.

"So, were you telling the truth?" she asked. "About maybe seeing me sooner than whenever Arlene chooses for the dress fitting?"

Ethan felt uncomfortable, but admitted he wasn't opposed to it. "If that's alright with you?" Still asking for permission instead of trying to take the lead. Even gods suffered from confidence issues, it seemed. He felt like a fourteen-year-old asking to hold his crush's hand while they walked home together, far from the prying eyes of their classmates.

Her wry smile returned. "I wouldn't ask if it wasn't, Ethan." His name sounded different in her mouth. As if it made him real, whatever that meant. "I'll be honest with you. I have a lot going on in my life. Like... *a lot*, and it's been enough to have to quit my job and move back home. It's been a very difficult few months." They hadn't really discussed anything too personal during the day. Just more feeling out, "getting to know you to see if you're a psycho or not", which was basically the state of the dating pool these days so far as he understood things. Her current hardships, whatever they may be, was all new information to him. She hid it very well, a skill he had not mastered. He wore his traumas on his sleeve like a four-star general.

"So," she continued, "I am raw, Ethan. Very raw. Raw and tired." From her lips to his ears. "You seem like a great guy..." Oh shit. No good news ever started with that sentence. "...but, and I'm sure you get this a lot... that plane thing."

Sunovabitch. "That plane thing" would be his actual epithet, he realized. "Here Lies Ethan Dessier. That Plane Thing". And that would be it. No dates. No heartfelt quote from a book he'd never read or song he didn't even like. Just "That Plane Thing", and that would summarize Ethan as a human being for the rest of eternity.

He understood, though. It sounded like she'd been through it a bit as well, and sometimes the last thing a person with drama wanted near them was a person with *more* drama. Like a pissing contest where no one wins and everyone is depressed.

"Yeah," he agreed. "That plane thing."

She looked at her house, a lovely place with a large yard that backed onto a small lake. Picture perfect. "Inside those walls is a lot of shit," she continued, "some good, some bad. So, which are you?"

The question came out of nowhere for him, and he didn't really have a great answer. Her honesty begat his, it seemed.

"I'm both. I kinda leave it up to the people I meet to determine which I am to them."

She didn't look back at him. He wished he could see what was going on in her head. Or did he? No, in retrospect he likely didn't. His head was full enough. "Did you have a good time with me today?"

"Yes." Not a lie.

"And you didn't drive all the way out here just because you thought I'd be good for a quick fuck and maybe a bit of fun between now and July and you can just wing your way to Spain or wherever whenever you want and I'm just your Chicago hook-up?"

"I'm not popular enough with the ladies in English. What chance would I have with European ones? I mean, have you seen my clothes?" If she smiled he couldn't see it, but Negative Nancy Ethan assumed not. "No, Vic. That's honestly not how I roll. I never have. I don't have the confidence or the constitution for those kinds of games."

She looked back at him. Scanning. Assessing. "And 'Marketing Company Think Tank' is your actual job?"

This question struck him right across the bow. Had he given something away? Lie? Truth? Lie? Truth? The choices people made in moments like this tended to define them.

"No. It's not. Not really. The travel and whatever is true, but no. It's a ruse to keep Arlene off my back."

No change in her expression. Her eyes reading him behind her glasses. "Why tell me that? You know I'm her friend."

"Because you asked."

She looked at her lap, pondering her hands. "If I ask you what you actually did for a living, would you say you kill people or something?"

Ethan had the ability to see a person's death coming, and in that moment he did not register his own impending end via heart attack. That was the only way he knew he wasn't about to die. After a moment he realized that she was just being facetious, creating some terrible job cliché as a joke. He couldn't bring himself to laugh. "I am employed. I travel to meet new clients and customers, and everything is legal."

It was a healthy mix of a lie and the truth. In her world, in the world they were both occupying at that moment, it was true. It didn't take an idiot to realize that that was going to bite him in the ass later, and he'd be nauseous with anticipation between here and there, but he let it rest there for now. It was the "Chekov's Gun" of relationship lies. If you say the lie, you need to expect the lie to return later.

"Saying 'everything is legal' is stupidly suspicious," she correctly pointed out.

"Extremely."

"Ok, one more question: tell me something about this afternoon you didn't like."

Oof, that put him on the spot. He didn't want to be a total ass, despite how on-brand that would be. He understood the question though. She was testing his integrity.

"I fucking hate squirrels. I hate them. I spent much of our time feeding them trying to ignore them while I stole looks at you and how much fun you were having doing it."

She considered this a moment. "That was it?"

In for a penny... "And checking you out. I apologize if that's rude. Not for some letch-y reason. Just..." Hmm, how to put this in a non-sleazy way. "...could I see us together. Even casually."

"And the verdict?"

"Pending, but promising. More in the green than the red."

She blushed slightly. It was so god damn enchanting. "I'll take that. You're pretty in the green as well, Ethan Dessier." His whole name this time, like his name in her mouth gave him substance.

She opened the door to the chill early-evening Indiana air. No hug or kiss. No physical touch of any kind. Just a look into his eyes. "Call me," she said. "And I mean call. Texting is so damn informal."

Despite his massive phone call anxiety, Ethan agreed. She pulled her phone out of her coat pocket. "Ha, speaking of." She showed him the lock screen. A multitude of texts had been received from Arlene. "Looks like she's checking in on us."

He went white. "You told my sister?" Ah fuck, he was never going to hear the end of this. Which was a stupid thought, really. Why the hell wouldn't she have told her? "Sorry, just little brother Ethan coming out. Of course you did."

"Of course I did," she confirmed. "I had a good time, Ethan. Thanks for coming out here for me. Give me a call soon, and Idunno... Let's just see, alright?"

Ethan agreed. "Let's just see."

The car door was almost closed when it sprang back open and Victoria popped her head back in the car. Ethan instantly thought it was some ambush kiss goodbye or something, and once again he found himself frozen, completely immobilized at the thought. It didn't happen though. "Tell me," she said instead, "because I'm going to lay awake at night wondering: what's the deal with squirrels? Is it a phobia or something?"

"Oh, no…" he replied, anxiety levels dropping rapidly. "It's just that a squirrel was really mean to me once. That bastard damn near killed me."

The weeks after their lunch date were perfectly pedestrian. At least, on the surface. Ethan called like he promised he would, and many texts followed as well despite them being so "informal", which was likely how she tried to get him to call and have a conversation. He couldn't say he blamed her.

His sister was all over him as well. As soon as he pulled away from Vic's house, a very succinct message appeared on his phone moments before he was planning on making himself and the black car vanish into the Everything.

"I will drop another plane on your fucking head if you screw this up and fuck up that woman or my wedding."

Ouch. Low blow, sis. Only she could get away with that.

Ethan was thankful for the slow, reasonable progression of his relationship with Vic. It made his professional issues much easier to focus on.

The rips and problems with various realities had only become worse. Before he was certain that although terrible, and of his own creation, these could be fixed. It was just going to take a shit-ton of blood and sweat before he got there, a penance for what he had done wrong.

Ever since the creature that had run wild in too-tall Chicago, followed by the algae of one world being shrunk and sucked into the core of an atom in another, more and more rips followed, and each one hit closer and closer to home until they could no longer be ignored: something was happening, and it might be because of him.

He handled it all as best he could, but he could feel the damage it was doing to the spectrum of light that he still viewed as an indicator of the general state of being. All light everywhere, and all pieces of light that bloomed from a dying soul worked to find a place and continue the cycle. That balance was being tipped, and when it tipped too far, the vacuum of the Nothingness at the End of the Tunnel would devour everything.

The most glaring incident came days before he was set to return to Chicago for another date with Victoria, and a week before the planned dress fitting at an upscale dress shop downtown. He had decided to have the date, and try to stay around the Chicago area for the week in case things went well and he could see Victoria again outside of wedding obligations. It was presumptuous, but that's just how desperate he was to escape the chaos he had created.

Ethan should have known it would all go south from there, but he never knew how bad.

In those days before the official "second date", he found himself adrift in what looked like an endless sea. The only reason he had focused on this one event was the nature of the one passing away.

It was a massive creature that came to dominate their particular area of existence, to the point where most life around it would grow or shrink in kind based on the state of the creature. Indeed, the "lone wolf" he had been hired to stop (and failed miserably at) was one of these kinds of creatures. He was a human-made-god, whereas this one was essentially a whale.

Well, sorta. It wasn't a whale like he grew up never giving a damn about (Sad but true. What did a kid from the suburbs of Chicago with a list of life issues a mile long give a damn about whales for?), but something more massive, in a vast and never-ending ocean on another world. It resembled more of the Moby Dick / sperm whale (*Wait, I just made that connection now. How the hell did I miss that comedy gold in grade school?*) as opposed to the humpbacks or blue whales of his home world.

This spectral creature was massive. Its skin pockmarked with barnacles large enough to create their own tiny ecosystems, and fish and plankton that followed it around like a submerged planet. The thing oozed life from every pore, and watching it move through the surprisingly clean sea it inhabited was something else.

It was also dying.

The death of a creature like this would be horrible at the best of times. So much other life encompassed it at all times, all relying on it in a gigantic, swimming symbiotic ecosystem. Its death would mean the death of millions of other creatures. It was a keystone. To remove it would bring a gigantic arch of life falling down.

That was a fact Ethan could not stop. That was why he was here. His bigger issue was that this massive creature, in its own understanding of the concept, didn't want to or plan on dying.

Much like Derek back before Christmas, this creature risked falling into Beneath. That would be horrible for both it as well as Ethan's consistently fragile mental state. The light of this thing's life was invaluable to him trying to balance things in the face of the rips.

Not to sound selfish but... wait, fuck that, selfish was exactly what he sounded like, and that's what he wanted! He needed this thing to die right. It had to know death was imminent. It was time to get to work.

He took his place in the background, probing the creature's mind to see where the issue could be. What did it have to live for?

The answer was as corny as it was sad: love. This big bulbous behemoth had been in love, and sired multiple broods. (*Atta be, big guy. Get that monolithic whale ass, son!*)

Sometime before, its mate had passed away. Ethan could remember it well now. It had been a task, but it went peacefully, surrounded by similar ecosystems, as well as some of its larger offspring, which then went out into this world to carry on their lives. This big guy had not seen that though, and it longed to find its lost mate. It knew it was dying, but it soldiered on, crying out for the one it lost. It had no concept of "death" per-se. It just knew it was slowing down, and that it was missing the one it wanted.

Ethan went to work, caressing the creature's mind, attempting to communicate the peace it could find if it just let go peacefully, instead of hoping to find its mate and swimming on forever until it did.

It was going well, until the rip.

A bubble of un-reality formed around the entirety of the creature, as well as the life that surrounded it. Where the bubble came from was a mystery, but it was empty. A void. Possibly just a pocket of space from anywhere or everywhere, and it proceeded to rip the creature and everything around it away, as if it had just randomly swum through a trap door in its reality.

"Shit!" Ethan cried out to the nothingness. "Not here! Not now!"

His words were meaningless. He quickly scoured the universes and at once discovered the creature, floating in space in a universe where time moved unbelievably quickly forward. The moment the creature appeared in it, its timeline zipped forward, and even Death itself couldn't react to something so unnatural in time. Before Ethan had a chance to try and set the creature on the right path towards finding the light, it was snuffed out unnaturally.

Ethan had no choice but to place the creature Beneath, eternally swimming towards a love it would never find in a painful reality of its own creation. Much of the life around it had to follow the same dark fate in its own way. Confusion at such a sudden change of reality did terrible things to life of any kind.

Ethan could only scream.

The void doesn't scream back. That made it the perfect thing to scream into.

The rip was massive, devastating, and for once he had to pull the dying light of other creatures not involved in the situation to fix it, with no way of knowing what the consequences were going to be. But the rip couldn't stay. The creatures were lost, their light unavailable for helping.

"Fucking. Hell," he said to himself aloud.

Moments later, he returned to one of his favorite places to think: the abandoned waterpark of his youth, floating in the vast everything of space. All water drained away, every pool empty. The scene beyond his little floating island of painful memories was the same as it was the first time he'd come here, full of stars and planets and nebulas of all sizes and colors. It was a visual representation of the vast everything that sustained life.

"Is this what you fucking wanted?!" he yelled. This space had come to represent his true beginning as Death. It was also where he went when desperate for answers. Or just to yell at reality for treating him so badly. "Do you want me to fail? Do you want me to actually put a bullet in my fucking head?!"

The last Death had tried to convince him to kill himself. Lately, he almost considered it. The thought of trying to fix all this just seemed so huge. So unstoppable.

There was no answer. Not that he expected one. The face-punchable visage of his predecessor didn't appear, and he was thankful for that. He had no one to be this angry at, and that fact just made him angrier.

It was so. Damn. Hard.

No, it wasn't hard; it was impossible.

He walked to the edge of the floating island and dangled his legs over the side. What would happen if he fell? What would happen if he let his human self just fall off and drifted in the void for a while? Likely nothing good.

No, he had to center himself. He had to find the key. However, his mind was so overwhelmed that he had a hard time focusing. Did meditation work for Death?

"We'll just see…" came a familiar voice in his head.

It was Victoria's voice that found him. Her voice, and that tantalizing promise of something profound with her that brought him back.

It was likely not very healthy to have that much faith in someone he hadn't known very long, obsessing like a BTS fan. Fuck it. Even if

Ethan hadn't been around her very long, anyone who had ever been in love could tell you that it was things like this that started it. Was he in love? Hell no. But the idea of something beginning with a woman who seemed to get him, or at least tolerated him, was enough.

Her face came to his mind. The rest was academic.

While focusing on that early-days relationship glow some people got addicted to, he reached out through the universes and found the rips that had happened, both large and small. It took a view that was multiple universes and realities wide to see it, but with enough focus, he got there.

The rips were radiating from Ethan.

They had been set in motion by the man-god in another world, but once started, it was Ethan that gave them whatever sustainable energy they needed to continue. How and why was beyond even him, and he couldn't feel out an answer to it yet, but when he looked at the vast tapestry that was what had been happening, he found himself in the middle of it. The incident with the sea creature was just the closest blow. A blow with some seriously poor timing.

He was the cause. He had apparently sent the creature into the Beneath with just his presence when it was dying. The guilt was palpable. So how did he become the cure?

How long had it been happening? He remembered the algae and the disappearing green from beneath the ice. That was pretty close. Hell, even the other-Chicago incident had happened in a version of Chicago not far from where he was, and only a few blocks away. The more he looked, the more it seemed that he was a magnet for these occurrences. If they weren't right at him, they were close enough, and getting closer. A dangerous consideration.

Well look at you piece it all together, Hercule Poirot. Turns out the murderer on the Orient Express may be you. What a fucking treat.

From the highest highs to the lowest lows, it sure had been a day, hadn't it. And now there was this to deal with.

One thing was for sure: Death was always exciting.

CHAPTER 10

"Two Truths and a Lie." She said the words like a business proposal, as if she was negotiating a deal between companies.

"I'm sorry, what?"

"Let's play Two Truths and a Lie. You first"

Ethan wasn't familiar with the game, but the title gave the rules away.

He and Victoria met as promised, this time at a humble burger place just outside of Valpo heading towards the lake. The place was mostly empty once more. It seemed Victoria liked late lunches.

She had hit him with the flirty game request the moment they had sat down. He hadn't even looked at a menu yet. Not that he really had to. It was a burger joint. Bacon cheeseburger, fries and a Dr. Pepper. The world over, it was his go-to. He would judge a town or country based on the quality of that exact order anywhere in the world, fair or not. Most universes were the same, but after he received a burger with meat that was still technically living in one world, squirming on his bun like a banana slug, he tended to keep his "classic" order to his own world.

Alright, it was game time.

"Hmm. Alrighty. Let's see..." For someone as worldly as he was, this should be easy. "I didn't get my license until I was twenty and just before the crash, my favorite coffee is Canadian, and Arlene and I didn't speak for two years after she left."

"Wow, bringing up the crash and a possible strained relationship with your sister in a casual get-to-know-you game. A bold choice."

"Well, I figure if you're going to assault me with a light-hearted game, I was going to make you squirm for it."

She looked thoughtfully at the table, then him, and then the table again. "It's tough. I'd hate to think my good friend Arlene could hold such a grudge, but it's possible I guess. Hmm. You're pretty good at this game."

"It's my first time playing."

"Bullshit."

He shrugged. "I wasn't terribly popular at the age where this kind of game would have been common."

She thought for a moment more. "The coffee thing. It's the most innocent and I think you're trying to be an ass, and I don't think Canada is known for their coffee, so that's the lie."

Ethan smiled. "I got my license the moment I turned sixteen. I was desperate to leave my home."

"Wow. Just wow. And now you throw in the damaged youth card as well. You really ruined this game, didn't you."

He blushed slightly, unable to tell if she was being sarcastic. "Sorry. It's in my nature."

"No, no not at all. I like it. Well, it's awkward and weird, but you sure don't disappoint when it comes to discussion topics. And the Arlene thing?"

He remembered that time in their relationship well. "It wasn't an animosity thing. She just got out and didn't want to look back. She'd later tell me the thought of talking to either of us was too painful. She apologized and obviously we're good now. Can't say I blame her. I wouldn't have wanted to talk to either of us either."

The server came by and grabbed their orders. He felt stupid, about to order something so basic, but when she led off with "Chicken fingers and fries please, and I'm good with just a water," he relaxed. She trumped him in basic by far with that one.

He made his order. "Pibb ok?" the server asked. Ugh. Dr. Pepper's gross doppelganger. *Don't be an asshole, Ethan!* "Pibb is fine, thanks."

Ugh. What a fucking lie. That was the worst complete lie he'd told in her presence yet.

"Alright, your turn," he said as they waited. She'd clearly been waiting and was on it like a shot.

"Sure. So, I have a twin sister, I'm allergic to the color red, and I graduated high school at sixteen."

"Ooo, a counter 'sixteen' question."

"What can I say, it's a pivotal age."

Ethan didn't think he was very good at this game, but his time as Death had taught him a thing or two about people. "Hmm." Was this considered fun? He hoped so, because that's exactly what he was having. After pondering the choices and using the open invitation to look Victoria up and down as if working something out, he thought he may have the answer. "I'm actually going to go with the sixteen thing. You know what? I'm going to double down: I think that's close to the truth. I think you were younger."

She didn't smile. Did he just suck the fun out of the moment? What the fuck was wrong with him! *Ethan: a man for all depressions.*

"You, uh, you nailed it." She didn't seem excited or surprised. There was a hint of worry in her voice now. What the hell had he done? "Um, how can someone with no social media be able to tell that much about me? Did you press Arlene for information or something?"

Ah, he didn't just suck the fun out of the room; he made himself look like some kind of creepy stalker. Time to see if the truth would set him free. "Oh jeez, that doesn't make me look too great does it? Mind if I dazzle you with a little sleuthing magic?"

"I really wish you would."

Good luck, Romeo! "Well, you haven't really mentioned much about your family at all other than your parents are still married and live on a lake. A sister is very possible, and even though twins sounds strange and impressive, it's not that weird in the age of IVF and whatever."

She still looked skeptical. "You're right. Non-identical result of a successful IVF. Go on."

Ok, ok, head is still above water. Keep treading, dummy. "The red thing was a bit harder, but I thought about all the meals or drinks we've had together. You never order wine or pop or cranberry juice or whatever. Usually water, or gin and tonic like at the engagement party. Drinks and candy are most likely to contain Red 40, a dye that can cause allergic reactions. I haven't seen you have any. You were trying to deke me out. You're not allergic to the color, but the popular food dye that makes kids with ADHD go bonkers, or so I'm told."

"Two for two. Makes me break out in hives."

"I'll remember that. So you know, cranberry juice is all natural. Just for future reference."

"I'll keep that in mind. Final round."

"Round for what?"

"To determine if I think you're an insane stalker and walk out of here."

Shit, no pressure. "Well, the last one is kinda on you." She raised an eyebrow. It was cute as hell. "You already told me you went to Purdue. That tells me you're pretty damn smart, because although your family has a nice house on a lake or whatever, it's still in Valpo Indiana. Comfortable, but not super-loaded, if you'll forgive me."

"Forgiven, but on thin ice."

"Then I'll step lighter. You got a scholarship, or at least a part of one. So, you're very smart. Graduating at sixteen isn't that weird for a smart, driven person around here."

"And why did you guess I was younger? Which is right, by the way."

"Well, the reasons I said above, but also, I hit you with multiple gotcha moments. Seemed fair you'd do the same."

To his credit, she didn't get up and immediately leave. "Pretty good," she told him. "Not one hundred percent, but a passing grade for sure. Actually, it kinda dovetails into my next topic of conversation, but we'll get to that in a moment."

Thank God. He wasn't just a pretty, stupid face! "Sorry if I sounded stalker-y. When you're the quiet one in the dark corners of any given room, you do a lot of people watching."

"Yeah, you really need to add more colors to your wardrobe. Goth and emo went the way of long sleeve shirts under short sleeve shirts a long time ago."

Ah, right. The black. A force of habit he would have to try and change.

Their food came and they both happily tucked in. The burger was... fine, it was fine. It was a burger. Rarely did a burger blow Ethan's mind, at least for good reasons. That was the joy of hamburgers. They were the great constant. Anyone over the age of eighteen was unlikely to say that "burger X is the greatest food I have ever eaten!". It was comfort food, but outside of some fancy, pretentious place that tried to slice razor-thin truffles onto a Kobe beef patty, it never strived to be in the upper echelons of food.

It was the "Ethan Dessier as a human" of food.

"So, what was that segued next topic you mentioned before?" he asked, taking another bite of delicious Mid-West meat mediocrity.

Victoria set her chicken finger down. "I was going to ask you if when we're done here, you'd like to come back to my place?"

Ethan immediately started choking. It seemed cliché, but the statement genuinely took him by surprise. He couldn't help but quickly inhale in anxiety as she said it, like a childish idiot.

"Whoa there, you ok?" she asked.

He regained his composure. "Sorry. Sorry. Just a crinkly pickle."

"Ah-ha, is that what you call it?"

Did she... did she just make a dick joke? Well played. "Sorry again," he deflected. "I was not expecting you to say that."

"Well cool your jets, lover boy. What I meant was, there's someone there I'd like you to meet."

He was genuinely baffled. "Parents?"

"Out of town for the night."

"I hate to say it, but 'parents out of town, come back to my place' is sure cause for pickle choking." And there they went. More words escaping his mouth without a leash and unsupervised.

The eyebrow was back up, but there was a smile on Vic's face. "Is that so? How about I clarify so you don't choke on another burger topping."

"Thank you. The lettuce was looking at me suspiciously."

"What I meant was," she continued, "would you like to come back and meet my sister? Sorry if that sounds too personal or like an ambush, but I think if you are honest in wanting to get to know more about me, she's the best place to start. I also trust her judgement more than anyone else on the planet. If you can survive her eagle eye, you're home-free from future suspicion on my part."

"A bold claim, but I accept the challenge." Holy shit, did he just agree to come home and meet the family? Or at least part of it? He even said it quickly and casually. Jeez, what the hell was wrong with him?

Victoria seemed just as surprised at the speed of the response. "Really?"

He knew he couldn't think about his response for too long, lest it raise more suspicion, but now that the words were out there he was shocked to find himself comfortable with the answer. Was this what being a deity did to a person? He hated it... "For real. I'd love to." Who the hell was this person speaking?! It sure as shit didn't sound like Ethan. Just how much did he like this girl?

Victoria had a small, soft smile. "That's great. Thank you."

Ethan could read the body language she was sending off. This was big to her. He still refused to probe the cosmos to find out why. Being himself and not the Caretaker of Demise had worked out alright for him so far. Best to keep it going.

They finished their "American Average" lunch and Ethan brought Vic back to her house, pulling up in the driveway. He escorted her to the door and stepped in behind her.

It was a classic Mid-West duplex. Some things reeked of the eighties like speckled ceilings and a giant "fuck-off" maple wall unit, whereas other things like the delightfully large flatscreen and occasional smart speakers listening to their every word but available to offer a quick kitchen timer placed the residents clearly in the here-and-now. A pretty standard dichotomy in today's world.

The house sounded empty. If her sister was here, she wasn't making a sound.

"One sec," Victoria asked him, and she slipped down a hallway. He could hear muffled voices, but not what they were saying. His superpowers remained safely locked away.

She reemerged and signaled him to follow. He wished he would have sent out a psychic ping, just once.

Down the hall and to the left was the master bedroom, but instead of containing a space made for her parents, there was her sister, lying in an at-home hospital bed, sitting up and looking at the door eagerly.

He stepped forward, hiding all signs of surprise. It seemed like a dirty trick to accost him with an ill family member, but he knew that game. As a kid, he never mentioned his mother and the state she could be in to potential new friends. It was like adolescent Russian roulette. Maybe she was sober! Maybe she was passed out in the yard! Spin the big wheel and find out! By the time he was a teenager, most people knew that you just didn't go over to Ethan's house, and he was fine with that. It gave him more and more excuses to leave.

"Ethan, this is my sister Laurel." He approached and took her hand, genuinely pleased to meet her. History and experience had taught him exactly how to react and be around people in her situation. He was basically the world's foremost expert.

Laurel was dying. There was no denying it. There was no chance at recovery. He didn't know the specifics, but he felt the aura of her situation and what it meant to his position the moment they touched, as he suspected it would.

She appeared taller than her twin sister Vic, though it was hard to tell with her lying down. She was dressed casually, but any exposed

DEATH AT A WEDDING

skin showed the telltale signs of someone who had gone twelve rounds with the worst the human body had to dish out and was suffering the consequences. She was pretty like her sister, but paler, and unnaturally gaunt. You didn't have to be Death to know that her clock was almost done ticking.

Unfortunately, he was Death, and that meant he could tell for sure. Why was he so fucking lucky. He tried to shy away from what he saw, knowing at this point that it wasn't imminent. He knew it was coming but didn't know exactly when. Not without a deeper look, a look he didn't dare take at this moment. He had to rely on his human side to do what he did best: break the ice and deflect the awkwardness.

"Laurel and Victoria. Sounds like someone's parents have an obsession with winning. I can relate."

Laurel laughed. It was a beautiful, strained sound, like a bird song from a distance you had to cup your ear to listen to. Victoria joined her.

"Yeah, that would be our mother," Laurel informed him. "She's pretty competitive."

"Is that why she had two of you at the same time?" Nice. Twin jokes. Very original, Ethan.

They both burst out laughing at the same time. "That's exactly what our dad says!" exclaimed Victoria. Ethan laughed along.

From there it was a walk in the park.

The room had everything Laurel needed without having to go too far on bad days. The on-suite, another large TV, and a sitting area with a desk and laptop beside the window that looked out over the backyard and the lake beyond.

It did not escape Ethan that this was likely an effort by her family to make sure she had a comfortable place to spend her last days. It was beautifully morbid, but Ethan really appreciated it. There were so many times he'd seen that families would fight and claw against a lost cause, dragging kids around the country to cure the incurable. He didn't blame them. Love was powerful, but it worked both ways.

Sometimes it would save a life, but other times it would just make it worse when all they really needed was a place to leave this world peacefully. It was almost impossible to know the difference. A painful truth.

They sat and talked for some time. Occasionally Laurel would ask Victoria for something and her sister would zip off to grab it, but for the most part Laurel just spent the time grilling Ethan, like a good older sister (by twelve minutes) should.

This was why Vic moved home and left her job, he surmised. *She came back to help look after her sister.* The master detective at it again. I was as honorable as it was heartbreaking. The human side of Ethan could not help but respect the effort, putting one's life on hold to help a loved one. God damn did it make him feel guilty as sin. He at least acknowledged that there was an ocean of difference between two close sisters making that sacrifice versus a young son for his mom, especially when the sister was just as nice as Vic was and Laurel's situation was an unfortunate act of God, and Ethan's mom was a drug-huffing bender queen. The expectations shifted drastically. That didn't change how he felt about himself, though. Humans gonna human.

At one point Laurel asked Vic to grab something a bit more substantial to eat, which her sister was happy to oblige. It was just Ethan and Laurel.

"So I appreciate your candor," Laurel said the moment Victoria was out of earshot in the kitchen, "but you don't need to be coy with me, Ethan. You seem like a decent guy, if not a little dour, but you don't need to tiptoe."

Ethan exhaled slightly. Addressing an awkward situation was preferable to dancing around it, he felt. "I appreciate you saying so," he answered, "but I don't mind. I know what it's like living with a tough situation. We can all be adults about it, but your situation isn't my business. I was just asked over to meet Victoria's sister. Whatever else is going on isn't my place to comment on or ask about."

Laurel smiled, but it wasn't a friendly or understanding smile. It was a mischievous one. He'd seen it on her sister's face more than once. "Well, I admit my personal situation isn't pleasant dinner conversations… Oh, by the way, did she even tell you what you were in for meeting me when she invited you over?" Ethan shook his head "no". "Ha, of course she didn't. Sorry about that. We've lived with it so long, you'd figure she'd get over the uncomfortable parts already.

"But that's not what I mean, Ethan. I mean you don't have to hide here. Not with me."

He looked at her questioningly. Something was wrong here.

"I know you, Ethan. I've known you the minute she showed me a picture she stole of you on her phone that first night at the engagement party." That tricky minx. He had no idea she'd done that. "I know who you are, Ethan. Or more specifically, I know *what* you are."

He expected something like this when he heard he was meeting a sister. She had some idea that he was a cad or lothario of some kind, no doubt. Hopefully he could persuade Laurel just as he was trying to do with Victoria. He was on the level, he really was!

"I know that you're Death."

Oh.

Oh hell.

Shiiiiiiiiiiiiiiit

He hoped and prayed that his physical body hid his shock well enough at being called out for what he was. It was a bold claim, and a strange one. You could almost say a crazy one. There had to be a sane explanation for it. "Death? Well, I admit I wear a bit too much black, but I…"

She held out a notebook that sat at her side. Inside it was a hastily drawn pencil sketch of a scene that made Ethan's blood go cold.

On the page was what looked like a massive sperm whale, surrounded by miniscule drawings of tiny life all around it. There was a strange bubble surrounding the creature, and outer space behind. The thing in the drawing was clearly long dead.

There was no doubt whatsoever that it was an image of the scene where he lost the whale creature to the Beneath.

What. The actual. Fuck.

Credit where it was due, Ethan had the ability to pivot in intense situations somewhat easily. A nature of the job, and his upbringing. He read the whole room right away. She called him out for what he actually was, and showed him a scene he couldn't escape. A lesser man would have denied and tried to gaslight such an impossibility. For Ethan, it was just another day at the offices of Barristers Strange, Twisted, and Bizarre.

"I fucking loved that whale. I really did. He just wanted to find his fucking girlfriend. Can you believe that?"

Laurel's hand started to shake noticeably, and her eyes went wide. "So, it's true?"

Ethan shrugged. "Well, you're the one who accused me of it."

"I just..." she stammered, "I didn't really believe it, you know?"

"Well, the whole truth is a bit more complicated, but you've done pretty well so far."

Seeing as she was already quite pale, he couldn't tell if she had gone more-so. He assumed she had. She'd apparently taken a long shot and actually hit the mark, and was now awash with what her accusation may mean. "So it's true?"

"Well, sorta," he admitted. He began flipping through more notebook pages. Each one depicted a drawing of a scene he recognized. The whale, the crystalline structure of the inner atom in space dotted with green. Even the tentacle monster. Page after page of similar scenes. All real, and all depicting a run-in with various dimensional rips. "I think you can understand that it's a bit more complicated."

"Yeah, I'll say." She motioned to take the book back, glancing down the hall for her sister. "Does Victoria know?"

"Victoria? Fuck no! Better question: how the hell do *you* know? It's not exactly public, as I'm sure you can understand."

Laurel turned the pages to something near the front of the book and then showed him. There were two images. On one side was an amazing recreation of Ethan's face, a dark hood around it, and frown he knew at once as his own. Like looking into a sketched mirror. On the other page was the half-smiling lips, piercing eyes, and horrible light hair of Death. As in, the Death who had recruited him. Squirrel-Death. That face filled him with more emotions than he thought he had in himself.

He scowled. "I really hate that man."

She politely took the book back, closing it while making sure Vic was still busy. "Who is he?"

He exhaled sharply. There was no precedent for this. No one had ever called him out before. He'd panic, but what did he have to panic about? What could one person do? Even if she told her sister, how the hell do you explain that? He was more exhausted than anything else. Just one more thing…

"He was my boss. The guy who hired me for the 'job', if you want to call it that. And he's a dick. I just want that upfront and on the record here."

"He doesn't look like it."

Ethan's eyes narrowed. "He didn't look like a lot of things. I just know what he was, and what he was, was a dick."

She placed her hands in front of herself, crossed slightly as if in silent prayer.

"Are you here for me?"

Ah jeez, that would break the heart of any sane human. How much did he say?

Just start with answering the question, he told himself. "No. I legit just went for lunch with your sister and she invited me back here to meet you. She said you were the gatekeeper of her virtue."

"She did not."

"Well, sorta. She said she trusted your opinion more than anyone else in the world. Same difference." Laurel blushed. The color bled through her pale skin.

"So," she began again, "I have a lot of questions. But most importantly: you're telling the truth? You didn't know about me and this was a surprise to you?"

Ethan nodded. "I'm not sure how much of the details I can give. Someone just blatantly calling me out isn't a standard occurrence, but as much as the word of some guy who just walked into your house and met you is worth, I promise you I'm telling the truth. I had no clue. I didn't even know she had a sister until lunch today."

"So, I'm special?"

"Pretty clearly, yes. Tell me, how long have you known this? That drawing of me and Ass McCockface there looks older than the month or so I've known your sister."

Laurel nodded in agreement. "Hard to say. I started seeing your face and these strange images on and off about three months ago. There was a flash of light and your two faces. What are the rest of those pictures?"

Three months ago? God damn it. Ethan was starting to get an idea what that was all about. The timeline sure did match up. That was roughly when, in this world, he had met the douche and lost. The images she drew all but confirmed it, because they all had a theme. "They're all things that have happened to me. Moments I've been a part of. Important ones."

He was afraid of a follow-up, but it didn't come. She changed directions. "Am I going to die?"

"Definitely," he said before he could stop himself. It wasn't a lie. He realized his mistake and countered quickly. "But you mean soon. I can't answer that."

"Isn't that what you do? If you are actually Death?"

She had no idea the breadth and scope of what she was asking. "Kinda. I don't think I can explain the finer details in the time it takes your sister to fix a snack."

Laurel looked back out the door. "So you don't plan on telling her?"

Oof. The gatekeeper of Victoria's virtue was testing the locks to make sure they were solid. "Well, the short answer is no, but the thing about me you need to know is that I may or may not be this thing you've accused me of, but I'm still Ethan Dessier. A living, breathing, overly self-conscious guy with a shitty history."

"Yeah, she told me about the plane."

"The plane is just for starters, but that's not a story I'm going to tell the sick woman."

She became sullen once more, again looking at her hands. "Can I be cured?"

Death Ethan sat forward, an honest look on his face. This was his job. His bread and butter. Mankind was notorious for shying away from death like it was a sketchy sex shop in the bad part of town: ignored, taboo, and better if not spoken about. It was an unhealthy and dangerous thing to do, in his opinion. Now faced with that human confrontation about the nature of what he did for a living (*Ha, did for a "living". That's fuckin' funny*), he answered exactly as he thought he would.

"No. But you already knew that. I can't see specifics until the time gets closer. Think of it like an aperture in a camera. It starts wide and then narrows as the moment gets near the end. Your lens isn't in focus yet, but it is there, and it is narrowing. I'm sorry. You just met me and I hit you with the bomb to end all bombs. Honestly, I just came to town for a burger."

"Why should I believe that?"

Ethan shrugged. "I don't know what else to tell you. You believe me or you don't. You tell your sister or you don't. You accept it or you don't. No matter what, I have to keep doing my job."

She thought about it, gave Ethan one more look-over, and then back down the hall where Vic was plating something and about to head back. "Can we talk about this again? Soon?"

Ethan's eyes went wide. "Yes please. I think that's a very good idea."

She leaned back as Vic entered, who set a tray on the bedside moving table with some soup and what looked like a cup of tea. She also brought a bowl of chips and set it on the desk between her and Ethan.

"What did I miss?" Victoria asked, likely seeing the flustered look on Ethan's face. No matter what he did, he doubted he could hide that. "What were you guys talking about?"

Laurel took a sip of tea. "Not much. Just getting to know each other. Mostly work stuff."

Vic's eyes raised. "Really?" She side-eyed Ethan, who hadn't given her much more about his profession since it was first brought up between them. "That's something I can't get out of him. You'll have to fill me in."

The look shot between Laurel and Ethan like a bullet. "Deal," Laurel smiled.

Ethan began to sweat. This wasn't how he planned his day to go at all. How the fuck had he missed something like this, with all of his cosmic vision?

Victoria saw the notepad at Laurel's side. "Oh hey, did she show you some of her drawings? I have no idea how she comes up with them, and she never really drew much until a little while ago. I sure as hell don't have that kind of talent. Aren't they amazing?"

Honesty is the best policy, Ethan. "V, they blew my fuckin' mind."

CHAPTER 11

The rest of the visit was painfully uneventful, as Ethan tried to wrap his head around the conversation he just had, and Laurel kept stealing looks at him like she'd just one-upped the Devil Himself. He supposed that in her mind, she kinda had. The terminally ill usually had a very good idea about what death was, but she was plugged in on another level.

When he could distract himself, Ethan was still mostly enjoying himself. The sisters were obviously best friends. Natural, considering their circumstances. When the evening set in and it was time for him to go, Laurel slipped him a note with her number on it so they could talk later. She had no idea he didn't need that. One quick peek at the connections within everything and he could just show up. Creepy and weird, but these were creepy and weird times.

He said his goodnights to Victoria and headed "back to town", but they agreed to meet up in two days for another long, late lunch. Ethan realized that Vic's proper lunch time was likely spent following a routine with her sister as far as making food or changing the bedding as needed. She was swapping in and out with their parents looking after Laurel.

Rearranging deck chairs on the Titanic and they fucking know it.

Now that he was free of his dating obligations, he was also free to investigate what the hell just happened, and if he was feeling bold, maybe try to determine what he was going to do about it. Baby steps, though.

The car evaporated into the haze of the evening as it drove along the interstate and Ethan got to work.

God damn it. How had he missed this? He had reached out to the great, vast everything and found the pattern in the rips, but hadn't gone further and figured out if there were other ones out there. Bigger ones. Smaller ones. Ones that took on different forms.

Ones that formed in people.

He figured that was what had happened. Laurel, for all the bad luck she'd already endured, had somehow become a conduit to a strange, unseen happening throughout the universes.

Now firmly plugged into the before-and-afterlife superhighway, Ethan probed the unfortunate woman that was Laurel. He found what he was looking for almost instantly.

There, buried in her recesses, mixed with the light of her existence, was a miniscule rip in space and time. It was almost camouflaged, blended in with the background noise of her existence. No wonder he had missed it, it was hidden so well. The strangest thing about this rip was that other than existing, it didn't actually seem to be doing anything. Nothing was passing in or out of it. It was essentially just floating there, a blip in a young woman that was ill, but was also hosting a tear inside herself, becoming a part of her.

Why was she so damn lucky?

Questions for another time, he supposed. Right now he had to try and fix this. Unfortunately, he had no idea how. In previous cases he could redirect or manipulate the essence of life to try and fix the holes, but she was still alive (barely), and the light inside her still held a valuable purpose. A purpose that even he could not interrupt. He guided the light when it was freed. This light was still active, working to sustain Laurel.

He also couldn't take the light of something nearby, like he had when trying to fix the damage done by the loss of the space whale. That was still freed light fixing a problem. This was a problem surrounded by active, vibrant light. He couldn't mix the two. The greatness of infinity tended to resist heavily when you tried to have two streams piss in the same toilet, as it were.

Damn it. Why did the world have to work against him so often? Forget Laurel; why was *he* so lucky?

He reached out closer, trying to understand the nature of what he was seeing. The rip was just kind of… there. Doing nothing horrible other than existing. Ethan could almost smell the aftereffects of his confrontation with the powerful one on the edges of the disturbance, mocking him and the choices he'd made. A reminder of a failure so huge, it had now infected the "soul" of a woman he had just met, and other than suffering from a terminal illness and all the baggage that had with it, she seemed to be pretty ok.

The further fact that she was the sister of a woman he was more than a little interested in, and the added knowledge that soon it would be his job to remove her from this world, certainly didn't help things whatsoever.

The joy of being a living Death, laid bare for all to see.

Ethan played with the problem in his head for a moment. It wasn't something that had ever happened before. Once more, just like remaining alive while in this position, he was breaking new ground, only this scenario held a lot more risk. In life, it apparently gave her the ability to see Ethan for what he was, and connect with many of the rips that had preceded her. In death, if she died peacefully, he could likely just take that moment to fix the hole and let her drift away like she was lost in the rock and roll.

A longer time in the command of Death than any creature in the history of existence, and Ethan still didn't have a damn clue what he was doing.

He didn't contact Laurel again right away. He had taken the week to be with Victoria and that was what he was going to do, damn it! The cosmic side of Ethan could keep up the good work, but the human side of Ethan had to focus on the lady.

Vic came into the city for their next lunch. Her parents were back and were going to look after her sister. This was how they balanced things, and Ethan had to respect the effort. This was how they kept their sanity in the face of impending tragedy, and it was working, as far as he could tell. Noble. Fruitless, but noble.

It was a Tuesday, and the core of the city was bustling. Victoria was worried they wouldn't find a place to eat, but Ethan had covered that base. And it didn't even require magic powers, which was good because he wanted to keep these interactions as human as possible.

Yeah, he says to himself just as he's finished probing the recesses of this woman's sister's quiddity. Just keep lying to yourself, you dumb schmuck.

Whatever. He couldn't listen to that part of his brain right now. He was Death, for fuck's sake. He could figure that out. The powerful feared him. Empires had crumbled because of him.

Well, his station. He still, even after all this time, even being the longest-tenured in the history of the job, felt like a child given the controls to a bullet train. He thought he should be the foremost expert on death by this point. Instead, he just tried to keep his head low and not fuck up.

Uh, again.

He had his sister book a table at a place she knew with a nice view of the lake, but also wasn't so uppity and pretentious that someone like Ethan would feel weird eating there. Ethan may *be* rich, but he sure as hell didn't *act* rich. Of course, Arlene's caveat to this arrangement was that she would be popping out from work and joining them, at least for the first part. Both happily agreed.

The three sat, Ethan with his cranberry and soda, the ladies with a drink of their liking, and had generally benign conversation about the dress fitting on the coming Saturday. That was, until Arlene finished her drink and looked to be ready to go.

Instead, she sat back in her high-backed chair like an adjudicator, eyeballing Victoria and Ethan. "Alright you two. I'm not leaving you alone until I get an answer: what the hell is this?"

Ethan spoke first. "Jeez Arlene, you can't pitch softballs all afternoon and then expect me to swing at the heat. This is lunch is what it is." Victoria said nothing, but pointed to him and nodded in agreement.

"Oh fuck off, both of you. If this 'thing' doesn't have a name, it's time you named it," she demanded.

"Name it? What is this, ninth grade?" Ethan deflected. He looked at Victoria. "Sorry, not to be the one to speak out here. Feel free to chime in."

"No no," Vic agreed, "lead the way. I'll tell you if you step in foul territory."

Ah shit. That wasn't good. She was letting him take the lead so that she could read his answers, and blow up if the need arises. The thing about wandering into foul territory in the early days of relationships was that unlike beyond the white line on a ball diamond, this foul ground was littered with landmines as well as the occasional random sniper in the stands. And he had walked right into this.

No small part of him thought this may have been planned. Fucking women. It was his own fault for getting Arlene involved. He literally could have taken Victoria for a meal on the Seine in Paris if he wanted. He even knew a place!

"So, there's your runway, kid," Arlene smirked. A plan perfectly executed. "What's going on here? What am I looking at between my good friend and my rotten brother?"

"Ouch. There's no need for name calling."

"I've called you worse."

"And I've deserved none of it." Silence for a moment, but Ethan could tell this wasn't going to just blow away.

Yep. It was a plan.

He suddenly felt like every eye on Chicago was looming over him. And then he looked at Victoria.

She wasn't as hawk-like and judicial as Arlene was being. She looked like she was an honest member of an impartial jury. Time to break out the dancing shoes. *Speak honestly, without giving everything away.* Honestly. He didn't know where that line was. He was almost as eager to hear the next words out of his mouth as they were.

"This," he began, heart racing as he looked at Victoria, "is the promising start of something incredibly good, incredibly real, and incredibly scary, between two people who likely don't have a fucking clue what they're doing…"

"Speak for yourself," Vic smiled

"Fine… at least, bare minimum, fifty percent of the people in it don't have a fucking clue what they're doing, but they're not scared to find out." The faint smile on Vitoria's lips almost melted his cold, jaded heart, but then he remembered exactly who he was. "And it will bloom, and grow, and flourish, and become something amazing, all in a coordinated attempt to ruin your wedding when the FBI busts into the restaurant because she and I are secretly planning a massive train robbery in an attempt to bring down Amtrak for their shitty times and horrible prices once and for fucking all!"

Victoria smiled wide, raising her glass. "Fuck you, Amtrak!"

Ethan continued. "Like, seriously. Guys will be swinging through the windows on ziplines and shit. Tear gas. One of those giant battering ram tanks you see in *Die Hard*. It's going to be so badass."

"Hey," Vic jumped, "can I drive the tank?"

Ethan leaned forward and took her hands playfully. "Oh you know it, baby. Anything for you. I'll crack out the ninja swords and karate chop them all and grab it for you."

"And we'll eventually go out in a hail of gunfire?"

Ethan nodded. "Bonnie and Clyde ain't got shit on us, girl. Just shootin' and swingin' swords and just blood, so much blood everywhere. Guests diving away left and right. Guts flying…"

"Alright!" Arlene interjected, already tired of the nonsense. "God. Fine, I'm convinced." She made a fake sign of the cross that Ethan was sure was some kind of first for her. "I hereby bless this fucking union. Just shut up about ruining my wedding already." Ethan and Victoria both just giggled. It was too easy.

Arlene grabbed her purse and coat. "And with that, I bid you adieu. Have a good time you two. I'll see you both on Saturday. You've got the address? That place in Sheffield?"

Victoria looked up. "You got it. We'll be there."

"Oh, it's *we'll*' now, is it?" Arlene raised an eyebrow. "How positively vomit-inducing." She smiled warmly. "Until then. Oh, and don't worry about lunch, it's on me." She turned and started walking.

"What? No," Ethan began protesting. "It's fine Arlene, you just had one drink, I can get…" but it was too late. Arlene just flipped him off with her back turned while she approached the hostess with her credit card out.

"Ugh, what a monster. Now she knows I'll owe her one." He looked down defeated, then up to Victoria. He was surprised to find their hands were still intertwined. "She is so fucking difficult sometimes. So, tell me, that was all a plan, wasn't it. A trap. An attempt to corner me to see what I'd say, yeah?"

Victoria's head nodded enthusiastically. "It absolutely was, yes. I deny nothing."

Ethan's head dropped, the defeats mounting. Beaten fair and square. "So how'd I do?" He looked up at Vic, eyes locked. It was an honest question.

Instead of answering, she crept towards him, her intentions clear.

Ethan was a coward for things like this, but seemed invigorated at her initiation. *Fuck it. Bombs a-fuckin'-way.*

Ethan and Victoria's first kiss was soft, trepidatious, wet, warming, and hit Ethan like a freight train right to the heart. It was two young people, with baggage and weights on their shoulders enough to fill a thousand planes to drop on unsuspecting gloomy millennials, connecting completely, and taking the first steps towards honestly and truly becoming something more together.

It was just cosmic coincidence that one of them happened to be the actual Specter of Death. No big deal.

They pulled away slowly, Ethan's head still swimming with hormones and endorphin rushes so strong he actually felt drunk. Victoria's eye remained closed a moment longer, as if she was savoring that same rush.

Ethan stole a glance sideways, to where Arlene had gone to pay.

Sure enough, there she was with the credit machine in her hand, staring googly-eyed at the two of them, her eyes big and her mouth locked in a silent "Ooooooooohhhhhhh" of pride and joy. Her head snapped to the hostess, and then back to them, and then the hostess again, where she suddenly mimed pointing at herself, and then them together, and then back to herself, clearly taking credit for this life-changing and super-charged emotional moment in her dark and broken little brother's life. She would be positively insufferable after this. The hostess smiled along, just happy to be part of such a sweet, silly moment on what was normally a boring Tuesday afternoon shift.

Ethan watched as Arlene left, floating on cloud nine and what she'd done just by proxy and the fact that she was getting married. It wasn't like she thrust them together or anything.

Ethan looked back at Victoria, who was staring unmoving at him. He suddenly felt very self-conscious. Damn it, why did she have that kind of power over him?! He was perfectly capable of making himself feel self-conscious without anyone's help! "What?" he asked. "Oh God, tell me I didn't screw that up."

"No," she answered, "you absolutely did not."

"Oh thank God. Not to out myself too much, but it's been a while."

"Yeah, same."

Their hands were still together, and stayed that way until their meals came.

They walked the streets of downtown after eating, not going anywhere in particular while they both basked in the afterglow only a first kiss can create. He couldn't speak for Vic, who was four and a half years older than he was, but he felt like a teenager again. Normally that was a terrible thing, considering what that time in his life was like for him, but here it was amazing. Amazing and terrifying.

Ethan had told her he was staying at a hotel nearby, a fancy one he would likely never actually stay in if he could help it. "It wasn't my idea, it was my boss," he'd told her, trying to impress while feigning being uncomfortable in such a place. *The peacocking never ends, does it?* he chided to himself.

"Yeah, I'm sure it's torture," she joked, her hand holding his, her body leaning close as they walked.

"So," he began, thinking of his next move, "are you around for dinner as well? Do you need a ride back or something? I admit I don't really have a plan here and I'm not sure what to do."

"That's basically the motto for my life," she said, slowing down. "Can I tell you something?" She stopped, pulling him out of the lane of oncoming pedestrians on the sidewalk.

"Sure, of course. It's not that I kiss like shit and you were just being nice, is it? I knew it needed more tongue! But when you practice on your closed hand there's zero creative feedback."

"Oh shut up! No, listen." She turned red at once. "I, uh, I may have told my parents I'd be staying in the city after going out with your sister."

He smiled a mischievous grin. "You lied to your parents for me? Well, now I'm convinced you're actually a teenager. Come to think of it, I've never seen any identifying information..." Reality dawned on him like a sledgehammer.

Oh.

Oh fuck.

Activate maximum anxiety! All thrusters to full! Blow the God damn ballast and surface! Oxygen! I need oxygen!

He looked at her, eyes wide as the pieces suddenly fit together.

Say something! Say something now or so help me God I will make you take your own life away! "I, uh, I think I'm not confident enough to make any kind of assumptions, so I'll just ask what you're proposing here?"

"I'm not going to have sex with you."

The hull just took a blow! We're taking on water! Red alert! Red alert! "Oh, I... uh... I have no response to that. Thank you for telling me?"

She steeled herself. This was apparently tough for her as well. He waited to hear what else she had to say, convinced this was going somewhere. "It's not that I don't want to. Stick that feather in your cap I guess." He would. He absolutely would. "I've just been burned rushing into these things before. I'm sure you have too."

"Uh, yeah…"

If she heard the sarcasm, she thankfully ignored it. "But what I'm saying is, if it's alright, can I spend the night? Grab dinner? Maybe a movie in? Curl up under the covers and you can keep me warm on a cold Illinois night?"

"Yeah, I'll tell you, I do *not* miss this chill…" He stopped abruptly, realizing this was not the time for casual weather chitchat. "Of course. I'd actually really enjoy that."

She relaxed. "Thanks. And you're not too disappointed? About the sex thing?"

"Did you just ask a virile twenty-two-year-old man if he was ok with not having sex?" Up went the questioning eyebrow again. "I am right there with you, V. Sex and I have a…" Broken? Practically non-existent? Laughable? "…complicated history as well. Let's do like you said. Besides, if you're honest about the kiss not sucking, I really doubt I could pull off two successful physical expressions of romance and desire in the same day."

She guided him forward again. "Well, I hope that's not true." He looked down at her, genuinely confused. "What?" she said. "Just because I said no sex doesn't mean *everything* else is off limits."

The hull is repaired! Only minimal damage detected! Stay the course! "Meaning what?" He was honestly curious. He needed to know exactly what he may be failing at tonight.

She stopped abruptly once more, pulled him down, and kissed him again. He practically felt his heart explode in a rush, and then she let him go just as soon as she'd grabbed him. "Meaning, let's find out what I mean, together. Sound good?"

It sounded good to him. It sounded very good.

She grabbed her car from where she'd parked it and they went to the hotel. The dinner was at somewhere less fancy than lunch but higher-scale than the burger place in Valpo. Because he'd been outright lying about the hotel he was staying in, Ethan had to quickly use his abilities as Death (albeit with extreme guilt about doing so) to manifest a room, as well as all the other little things like a suitcase and toiletries in the bathroom. He didn't want to risk giving anything away. Not yet.

Tick tock, dumbass.

They went back to his room, which she agreed was fancy and not really his style, but otherwise didn't complain about the luxuries as well as the view of Lake Michigan. They eventually dressed for bed, curled up together, and started the movie.

It didn't even make it to the title card and they were all over each other, with a fresh, exploratory passion that neither could fake even if they tried. They spent the next few hours finding out exactly what she'd meant by "other things were not off limits", and Ethan enjoyed every single moment of it.

Just past midnight, mostly naked and completely spent, they went to bed properly, with Ethan's arm around Victoria's cool, exposed shoulder. He laughed quietly to himself.

"What?" she asked sleepily. "What are you laughing at."

"It was Arlene," he said, "she is absolutely going to take all the credit for this."

"Oh whatever. It was just chance we were both at that party. If anything, it's Laurel who should be congratulating herself."

Ethan pulled back and looked at her, suddenly very interested and awake. "What do you mean?"

"I mean, she was having a really hard time the day of the engagement party. I told Arlene I was really sorry but I wasn't going to make it. I had to be there for her. But Laurel insisted I go. That's why I was late that night, because I was so damn stubborn and refused. She fought me tooth and nail to make sure I did. I'd never seen her so adamant. She said I had to. She said if I didn't get out and enjoy myself that night, I may miss out on something amazing, and that she loved me but she'd feel terrible if I missed it because of her." She turned over, pulling herself up to meet Ethan face-to-face. "I thought she meant seeing my old friends and having a good time for once since I'd been so wrapped up in looking after her." She kissed him lightly, a sweet, soft peck. "I never for a moment thought she meant meeting you."

She resumed her previous position, cuddling into Ethan's chest. Moments later she was asleep.

Ethan had never been more awake in his life, and as much as he hated to admit it while lying in bed, emotionally and physically satisfied as he'd ever remembered feeling in his life, he knew exactly what he had to do, and it pained him.

He needed to talk to her sister.

Right now.

CHAPTER 12

She had to fight to get to the washroom, and it pissed her off so much. Each step hurt, and that was likely just going to be the beginning of the uncomfortable moments as she got ready for bed. It was late, but she barely slept regularly anymore. It was more of an hour or two up, an hour or two asleep, repeated throughout the day. Day and night was all a mishmash, and it upset her that this strange cycle of confusion and exhaustion would likely never change for the rest of her life, whatever was left of it.

Cancer fucking sucked.

Her nighttime routine was constant, but every day brought a new adventure. Maybe she'd have trouble going to the bathroom. Maybe her teeth would hurt when she brushed them. Maybe the sensation of water in her mouth would make her want to throw up. It was like a spin of a terrible wheel of prizes.

She'd get through it, though. As long as she could. She wasn't a quitter. Even when she had faced Death himself (apparently) and received a clear answer about her fate, her will would milk every day it could out of this existence, and then, she would just have to see what was next.

When the deeds were done and she escaped mostly unscathed, she slowly went back to her bed to get whatever sleep she could before her body decided it wanted to complain again. She had only sat down for a moment when she saw him, shadowed and relaxed in the desk chair across the room, apparently looking out the window at the reflection of the moon on the ice-covered lake. She startled, scared at the appearance but unable to react with anything more than a sudden shock and a voiceless yelp.

The shadow turned and leaned forward, pulling back their black hood.

Death had come for a visit.

"If it makes you feel better, I waited until you were done in the bathroom and then sat down. I didn't want to scare you into falling or anything."

She recognized the voice, even if the face was obscured by darkness still. She pressed a button at the bedside and a lamp illuminated the room with a soft glow. "Thank you. I appreciate that. How did you get in here?"

Ethan smiled. "Asks the person who knows my dirty little secret. I'll tell you something you may not have realized: Death is truly everywhere."

Something dawned on her in the moment. "Wait, aren't you spending the night with Victoria?"

Ethan looked guilty at once. "She, uh… she told you about that?"

Laurel raised her eyebrow, just like her sister but far less cute when it was clearly meant to call Ethan a fool. "She lies to our parents because they're kinda old-school, but I'm sure not. Are… are you with her right now? Did you pop into my room right after having sex with my sister?!"

"No!" Ethan defended at once. "Well… sorta? We didn't have sex! I'm… jeez… it's complicated. I'm there, but I'm here as well. I'm kinda everywhere? I'm not getting into it. She's asleep beside me right now, but I don't really sleep and I saw that you were up and I thought it was about time we spoke because of something she said and…" Laurel watched him backpedal with a certain amount of interest. Time for a new tactic. "Hello, I am Death, and I've come to have a conversation with you about our interconnected situation."

"Did you guys have fun?" she smirked.

"Death is not getting into a conversation about what it may or may not have done with your sister."

"Whatever," she replied, "just don't screw it up. She deserves all the good things."

Ethan looked at her with a deeper interest now. "You... you don't seem to have an issue with the fact that your sister is currently in bed with Death."

She shook her head. "No, she is currently in bed with a guy named Ethan somewhere in Chicago. Death is here visiting her dying sister. Does that sound about right?"

"Close enough. I still have to say I'm a bit on edge about how casual you're treating this."

She leaned into the bed, its back rest elevated at the moment. "Has anyone ever met you in a non-work-related capacity?"

He laughed to himself. What a story that was. "Yeah, *I* did. I was apparently the first. I believe you're the second." She looked at him, her eyes demanding more of the story.

In for a penny once more, big guy!

He proceeded to tell her the story of how he'd got the job. The meeting at O'Hare. The Puget Plunge* (* - Copyright renewed due to returning interest by the public). The man who was the other picture she'd drawn (leaving out no details about what an asshole he was).

He then explained as best he could his encounter with the man-god in the other world, what had happened there, and how he had failed, as well as how that failure had exacerbated the appearance of the rips in space and time, creating the problems he'd had and the drawings in her book.

She sat quietly, listening intently, occasionally taking a sip of something from a cup beside her. When he was done, she remained silent, taking everything in. Eventually she took the book from her bedside table and held it up. "And you think one of these rips is inside me?"

"I know it is. I've seen it myself. There's no doubt. It's kinda acting like cable TV, showing you other rips and what's happening with them."

She lowered it. "You were inside me?"

Uh-oh. Keep digging, shithead. "That sounds a bit more invasive than I'd prefer."

"I'll say."

"But, it was actually a big help. If I didn't do that, I'd never known what the fuck was going on!"

"So this is all your fault." An accusation, not a question.

His head bobbed back and forth. "Yeah. Well, sorta. The cancer's not. That's just nature being fucking nature, warts and all. But the visions and the ability to see through my dashing disguise? Yeah, that looks like it was all me. Sorry about that." The apology was genuine.

More silence for a very long time. He did not envy everything she was trying to take in right now. He knew the feeling.

Eventually, he had to speak up. "Look, I need to ask you something. It's about the night Victoria and I met." She said nothing but indicated he could continue. "She told me she was going to stay here with you, but you basically kicked her out. Why?"

She crossed her arms, leaning her head back completely as if lost in thought. "Ah, yeah. That day. It was a bad day for me. Like, really bad, but I wouldn't let her stay. I knew she had to go. I didn't just want her to, I *needed* her to, you know?"

"I'm afraid I don't. I can't see those kinds of things. I show up after the show is over, rarely when it's happening."

"Except when a lady is using the bathroom."

He held up his hands defensively. "Hey, I said I waited, I swear!"

She smiled and continued. "I just knew she had to be there. It was a feeling I can't explain. As strong as an emotion instead of an opinion. It was almost primal. And it seems to have worked out, right? She met you there, though now I'm not sure that was a coincidence. It was more like…" *Don't say it, don't say it, don't say it…* "Fate." *Ah fuck, she said it.*

Ethan bristled. "I'm afraid I don't have much room in my life for fate, Laurel."

She looked back at him, curiously. "Really? And you're Death?"

"Last I checked."

"Huh, well I officially have no idea how the world works."

Ethan manifested a glass of water and then took a sip. "Well that makes two of us."

She looked at the cup, and then back at Ethan. "For what it's worth to say this to Death, I still think it was. What else could it be? Coincidence seems like a stretch."

"Coincidence is another word for fate."

Her eyes went to her hands. "I'd feel better if I could believe it was. I need something here. If not for me, then for her. She's been through it. I'm not sure what she's told you, but she has. I guess you're Death and you're everywhere and you know all or whatever."

"Nah, I know what I need to know. I don't pry into lives. It's not my place. Call it a human weakness in an inhuman force."

She smiled softly. "That's good to know. Even with unlimited power, you still seem like a decent guy."

"I'm just a guy in a unique station. I've made mistakes. I've done things I regret. And I've used my office to do stuff I don't regret at all. The human element only complicates things."

"I'm sure it does." The smile faded. "It's getting late. Can we talk again? Soon?"

"For sure. I've got your number."

"Apparently you don't need it."

He shrugged. "Perk of the job. That and bottomless coffee."

"Ugh. God I miss coffee." She sighed. It had been so long. "Wait, I can have it, can't I? The doctors said to avoid it, but you already told me there's no way out of this."

"I'll leave that choice to you, lady. I don't know when, and if your will is strong enough, it can tilt the scales for a bit more time. It did for me."

"Right, but unlike you, I can't escape?"

"Like I said, nature's gonna nature. I'm sorry. My situation was different. Different, and damned if I still didn't fuck it up."

She looked at him thoughtfully. "So, if you didn't 'fuck it up' as you say, you likely wouldn't be in the job right now, and wouldn't have met my sister because I never would have sent her to that party. Doesn't that sound like…"

"Nope! No, I'm not getting into this. I'm going to go back and defile your sister just to spite you if you say that 'f' word one more time."

She smirked. "Oh I feel like that ship has sailed." The soft smile again. "Thanks for coming by. Is it weird that it makes this whole thing easier because I actually get to talk to you?"

"No. No, actually I'd say that's quite a perk for you. I wish I could interact like this with more people. It would make death a lot less scary."

"It is still scary. But I appreciate you saying it's not. Good night, Ethan."

Ethan replaced his black hood. "Yeah, you too. I'll see you soon." He suddenly realized the implication of his words. "Not, like, for work… I'll see you to talk about the rip thingy… until it *is* for work… god damn it I hate talking to people!" And with that, he disappeared.

Morning in the overly fancy hotel room started with a kiss, a snuggle, a coffee, and a decidedly rated-18+ co-ed shower, followed by breakfast, before Victoria said she should be going home. "I'll see you Saturday?"

Ethan looked at her as she got into her car. "And miss an opportunity to make fun of my big sister in fancy dresses? You couldn't keep me away."

"Oh be nice. She cleans up pretty well when she wants to."

"I'll take your word for that, by which I mean I think you're lying."

A quick kiss and she was off. Ethan Dessier did not deserve to feel as happy as he did.

Now "back to the office" as it were, he had time to focus on the Laurel problem.

Because of the rip, she had an insight no one else had. Because of that insight, she now knew Death personally. Because she knew him personally, she could ask if she was actually going to die, and if she could do anything about it. Now she knew that the answer was yes and no, so there wasn't much risk of her denying her end and going to the Beneath. Who knew what the hell would happen if a rip got into there!

Honestly, other than the fact that she was the sister of the girl he was apparently dating (*Weird! That sounded weird!*) it couldn't have happened in a better way and to a better person. Which ironically, also really sucked because that meant a good person was dying and there were hard times ahead because he knew Victoria was still holding on to some faint hope Laurel would pull through.

A quandary for sure.

Work went about as usual for the next two days, and he didn't get any closer to figuring out why Laurel was the lucky victim of circumstance. He'd never met her, didn't know her, and had no connection to her.

No. That wasn't true. She was the sister of a friend of his sister. It was a loose connection, but it was basically one degree of separation in this world, which was a mathematical impossibility. Millions and millions of worlds out there, and it was someone in this one, his home world, with that close a connection to him, that got dealt the Joker? No way that was random.

Just more fucking mysteries. God, he hoped nothing would happen to Victoria.

Speaking of, both she and Arlene let him know they'd meet him at the bridal shop, as "the girls" were going for breakfast and it was strictly no boys allowed. Fine. He didn't want to be in on that hen party anyway, as each of them likely clucked and pecked away at his and Victoria's relationship. Gross. Gross and awkward. Then they'd start talking about dick size or whatever and then he'd have to shrink into a pit and die. At least he assumed he would. Best not to find out.

He apparated a few blocks near the shop and hoofed it from there. Even Death needed a bit of fresh, cold air and exercise now and then.

He made it to the place, a little brick building in a nice, urban, white bread part of town. Serviceable, but not his usual cup of tea. An Uber pulled up a moment later and the four ladies jumped out, full of morning cheer (at the very least).

He had done himself up at least somewhat. The long black coat over what could graciously be called dark gray jeans, and an actual button-up shirt to top it off. Why was he dressing to slightly impress?

When he caught a clear look at Victoria coming through the door with her friends, the answer was clear.

Fucking hell, you've been around women before, you know. Do you think this shitty display of mild personal grooming will do anything for you?

He wasn't sure, but it was too late for it now. They were already in, all eyes on him at once as he sat in one of the fancy chairs surrounding the elevated platform where Arlene would be trying things on. Jesus, it was all just pageantry, wasn't it. He prayed he never had to go through this kind of thing.

He said hello to the other two (*Rachelle and Lisa? Liza? Laura?* He was terrible at names. *Looks like I'll need a quick scan of the universal Rolo-death so I don't like an ass and... What the... Tara? Man, I was way the fuck off*) and greeted Arlene and Victoria, respectively. Every single one of them giggled upon seeing him and shot each other a quick glance while pointlessly trying to hide their smiles.

Yep. Talkin' dick size. I fuckin' knew it.

Whatever. He wasn't going to be intimidated by this crowd. He was the commander of the afterlife, damn it! He stepped to Victoria and went to kiss her, which she eagerly jumped at (much to his relief) planting a soft, wet one on him. "You look great! You almost wore a color!" she said, pointing to his jeans.

He could taste the ice wine on her lips. Whatever. He was glad she had fun. However, now was time for *his* fun, and once they settled in and their "Personal Attendant", as she was called, had given them something else to drink, the show began.

Seeing as it was meant to be a low-key affair, there were none of the usual Disney-style flowing gowns with trains from here to out the door. It was closer to fancy cocktail dresses, with mid-calf hems and pencil cuts. Hardly worth his participation, honestly. There was little room for screw-ups with these. However, now that Victoria was in the mix, chatting and laughing with her friends, he found that he was still happy to be there. Once Arlene started asking his opinion on things ("It's why I wanted you here, ass") he began to loosen up. If she wanted honesty, he'd deliver.

The lacey one with the rose highlights?

"It's alright. And hey, if you ever wanted to blend in at an old lady's house you could just quickly lay down on the top of the plastic-covered furniture."

The longer one with a matching shawl and clutch?

"It's not bad. You don't in any way look like you're trying to hunt down one hundred and one dalmatian puppies."

The a-line floor length chiffon with the high leg slit?

"Oh my God I had no idea you were a professional assassin! Toppled any foreign governments with a sultry tango lately?"

What about the pixie silk mini?

"Ok, save that for the wedding night, and I never want to see that much of your skin again."

And the v-neck jumpsuit with wide legs?

"Look… I mean… I'm the one who has to walk you down the aisle here. Are you even thinking about me when you pick these? You look like a random pile of cocaine in the bathroom at Studio 54 in 1978."

The girls all took his shots with good nature, a perk of being pre-introduced as a douchebag, but eventually the day went on and everyone was getting hungry again.

And then the long halter-top dotted with crystals around the neck with the open back came out.

The girls instantly went mad, each proclaiming she'd found the one for sure. However, Arlene's eyes fell on Ethan. Soon so did the eyes of the other three. Wow, he had no idea he held this much sway. He was convinced he was here for moral support more than anything. What made any of them think he had anything resembling taste when it came to these kinds of things?

"That," he said very point-of-fact, "does not suck."

That was all that was needed, as the attendant got the thumbs up and then whisked her away for the proper measuring.

Victoria leaned over to him. "That was a great choice. Who knew you had an eye for that kind of thing."

"Well I sure as shit didn't. I'm glad she's happy, though. Hey, what are you three wearing?"

She smiled. "You'll see."

There went that heart melting sensation again. He prayed it would never go away.

A short time later Arlene reemerged and the bridal crew headed out. Arlene gave him a big hug. "Thanks for being here. I really appreciate it."

"Hey, you ask, I deliver. That's how amazing I am."

"Do you mind if I steal your woman for the rest of the afternoon?" If he was being honest, a part of him did mind, but that was just selfishness on his part.

"Not at all. Have a blast, ladies." They piled into the car, with Victoria promising to talk to him later.

The window rolled down and Arlene leaned out. "Oh, hey, we also need to talk about what you're going to wear. I had some ideas."

He looked down at himself in mock surprise. "What? What's wrong with my style? You don't trust me?"

She rolled her eyes. Man, when someone did it to him it was really annoying! "Whatever. You dress like you're always on your way to a hobo's funeral and you know it. Today was only a marginal improvement. Big steps need to be made."

"Ugh. You're not going to make me wear a tux, are you?"

She looked up to the sky innocently. "Maybe. I'll make you wear whatever the hell I want. It's my wedding. You'll walk with me wearing nothing but black boxers and a bow tie if I ask you to. I know *some* people in this car who wouldn't argue!" Vic wrapped Arlene on the knee with minimal force while she blushed. "I'll talk to you soon.

Love you, bye!" and she was back in the car, off to cause whatever mid-day, upper-middle class shenanigans women got up to these days in Chicago in February.

"First official wedding duty completed successfully," he said aloud to himself. He was almost proud he didn't completely screw it up.

CHAPTER 13

The early days of love are about the hardest interhuman interactions a regular person ever needs to go through. So much time is spent just trying to figure out if something is real or just a brief hormone rush, and that was the kind of thing that could really throw someone for a loop. Is it something real? Is it something that can blossom and turn into something more? Was it just a passing thing, a relationship brought about strictly by circumstance? The ability to determine these kinds of things usually made or broke the connection between two people in the early going.

For someone who also happened to be Death, The Stranger at the End of the Path, The Dark Man, The Keeper of the Universe's Secrets, it was exactly zero percent easier, a fact that frustrated Ethan to no end.

February turned to March, and then April, and the weather went from wet and cold to wet and slightly less cold. Arlene would consult with him when a guy's opinion was needed, and they had lunches and dinners and moments together just enjoying the only family each of them had.

Arlene would grill him on Victoria constantly, and he knew she was doing the same on the other side of that coin. That's what big sisters were for. She had never really been this close before their mother died, even when he moved out, but ever since the plane crash and Ethan's subsequent disappearance while Death showed him the ropes, she had become dedicated to making up for lost time. He didn't mind. He appreciated the human connection. Maybe, just maybe, the two of them could make it out of this world without more surprises.

As for Victoria, Ethan was basically on eggshells all the time, terrified of giving away his secret, despite knowing that the day would come. He'd seen enough romantic comedies to know that someone as clueless about relationships as he was had no chance in dodging that bullet. In keeping his human, living side, he had basically kneecapped the role of Death. His refusal to delve deeply into the lives of Victoria or her sister, or anyone really close to him, was likely a poor choice, but he refused to change it. Yeah, he could spy on Vic naked in the bathtub whenever he wanted, or make the greatest gifts in the world appear and hand them over to her, but his humanity is what made him who he was in this role. It was because of that that he was here.

Laurel had alluded to it, but it was incredibly lucky that because of his job, he had met Vic. Not fate. Just lucky. That was the only explanation he could accept. Sometimes it was better to be lucky than good, and Ethan had never really been either, so he just took it and let it be.

Speaking of Laurel, he was true to his word and made more visits. She was a nice person, and it was a shit deal that she was in the state she was in, but that's how life worked, and the faster people realized it the better and fuller their lives would be.

She stayed in tune with the rips and the scenes they created. It was refreshing for Ethan to have someone he could discuss them with. Before he knew it, and ashamedly behind Victoria's back, they had actually become friends. It broke the human part of him to reappear after a few weeks and see she had deteriorated in health. That focus was getting closer, and in his expert opinion it looked like it may just close sometime in the summer.

Like, say, around Arlene's wedding.

Of course. Of course it would. That was just how these things worked with him, wasn't it. He had faith in Laurel that she'd push herself as far as her will would go to let Vic have her friend's wedding to have some fun, but some things she just didn't have a say in.

Things had gotten particularly bad as spring came in full. The work her body was doing was not enviable at all. She would fall, or pass out randomly with little or no warning. She was constantly monitored now, and she would be until the end.

Ethan's inability to see just how closely she was being monitored due to his refusal to be more than Ethan Dessier to Victoria and Laurel was exactly what caused the issues that changed everything.

It was another fun night in downtown Chicago for him and Victoria. The kind of night that made him thankful he had lived through a giant tragic plane crash, even if billions of lives had suffered because of it in the long run. It was selfish, but fuck it, he deserved to be selfish sometimes. Even with that crash, his life before Seattle was not in any way enviable, and he suspected the same went for her, though he still didn't pry. It would come. He had all the time in the world.

Or so he thought.

He would say he was traveling around the world, bring her a trinket from Tokyo or Madrid or wherever (which to be fair, he did actually get from those places). They were celebrating his return from Australia with a *Crocodile Dundee* double feature in the hotel while he pointed out the numerous factual inaccuracies of Aussie culture.

"Like, honestly," he asked while she was curled against him under the covers, "was the 80s just movies about stereotypes? Things like this and *Short Circuit* were just so cringy."

"Hey!" she protested. "What's wrong with *Short Circuit*? I loved that movie!"

He side-eyed her. "Have you seen it lately?" She admitted she hadn't. "Well let's just say the Simpson's Apu controversy with Hank Azeria has *nothing* on Fisher Stevens!" One quick search on her phone confirmed that although the robot was cute, that movie had not aged well.

"How's your sister?" he asked casually partway through Part Two.

In truth he knew exactly how she was, but he wanted to hear what she had to say.

"Not great," she admitted, "she's falling more, and is losing her appetite. The doctors prescribed her more medicines, but at this point I'm afraid she's taking one step forward and then two back."

"I'm really sorry to hear that," he said honestly. "Is there anything else anyone can do?"

Victoria was quiet for a moment. "No, not really," she said eventually. "It's up to her now. We've done some stuff around the house for her to help out. Some things she honestly doesn't even know about, but we were afraid if she knew she'd get mad, and we didn't want that. You need to weigh these kinds of things very closely, you know?"

If only he had been more curious. If only he had dug a bit more into that statement instead of passing it off as a sister talking about ways to help a twin she loved more than life itself.

If only...

Much like the first time he'd done so, he waited for Victoria to fall asleep, and then he checked in on Laurel. She was awake, but just sitting in bed. Her drawing notebook was off to the side of the bed. She still loved to use it to draw the visions she shared with Ethan, but her hand needed more and more breaks, which she was taking now.

"Oh, hey Ethan," she said as he slowly appeared at the foot of her bed, her voice weak. "I wondered if you'd come by tonight. It's a lot like that first time, isn't it."

"Yeah, it is. I guess that's why I thought of it. I hope you don't mind."

"Well, it is kind of weird you like to stop by after boning my sister."

"Oh whatever. First of all, you know we haven't had sex and don't act like you don't. Second, who the fuck calls it 'boning' anymore? This isn't a nineties frat comedy, jeez."

"Yeah, sorry, that was a stupid word, wasn't it. Still, it's weird. Thanks for coming, though."

"You're welcome. She was talking about you before she fell asleep. That also made me think I should pop in. Said things had been harder lately."

She started coughing violently, as if the words had summoned the phlegm. "Yeah," she choked out at last, "you could say that. How's that camera aperture look now, huh?" She smiled faintly.

"Closing, but you don't need me to tell you that. How do you feel about that? Are you okay?"

"No," she answered quickly and honestly. "No, I don't want to fucking die, but that aside... I'm getting there. You've been a big help. I'm glad you've been able to help me, even if it's reluctant."

"It's not reluctant, just confusing. I don't get what's going on or why, but I'm glad I've been able to add a ray of sunshine."

"Ha," she pitifully laughed, "I wouldn't go that far. Would it kill you to wear a color sometime? For someone who's trying to help me and make me feel better, you could show up, you know, not looking like Death all the damn time."

"Sorry, habit of the job. And the depression. We can't ever forget the depression."

He had told her about his upbringing, sparing some of the worse details since she was already going through enough.

"So," she said, changing the subject, "that last rip was a crazy one, wasn't it? How did you fix that?"

The rip she was referring to was a strange one. An extremely long hole many miles wide but infinitesimally thin had torn across half a distant solar system, causing planets to lose chunks of themselves and obliterate the small, cellular life that had formed on some of them. In the end he had to take some of the fading light of life and spread it thin across the rip like glue on a wound. The problem with that was that he wasn't sure how long something like that could hold. It would have taken an insane amount of light to fix it fully. He was afraid it was going to tear open again. So far it hadn't, but he was monitoring it closely until he could find a more permanent solution.

"Seems like a quick fix. You may want to get on that," Laurel had said when he explained it. He totally agreed.

She yawned, a clear indication she was fading for the night. He didn't want to keep her. Before she kicked him out, she asked an interesting question. "Hey, I had a thought: you know how you got this job from someone, and it keeps getting passed on like the title of Dread Pirate Roberts?"

"I do, and I also appreciate the reference. Great movie. Go on."

"Well," she said, the bed now moving backwards into a sleeping position, "maybe that's what you're doing with me? Maybe that's why I'm so plugged in? Maybe I'm next in line?"

The great Powers That Be still hadn't answered his call to find out how to pass this job on, and the rips and tears had continued with no sign of slowing down or ramping up. Just inconveniences that tipped the balance here and there while he scrambled to fix the problem he had made.

Her thought was an interesting one, but it was also one he had considered already. "No. Not to be blunt, but I've given that some thought and already ruled it out. I've scoured every bit of what makes you, you, and although you're a great person who was dealt a shitty hand, you're not a Deathmore."

"A what?"

Ah, right, he hadn't brought that up yet. "Deathmore. It's the name of those that get the honor of the title when the time comes. You're a strong person, Laurel, and I'm positive you'd make a great Death, but that's not your part in this."

The bed down completely now, he went to her side. "It's for the best," she seemed to agree. "I may be good at it, but I doubt I'd have the constitution for it. How many innocent people or babies or distant lifeforms who could have done great things have you taken?"

He dropped his head. "Enough."

"Right. Well, I'll leave that with you, and I'll just plan on painting the stars with my light."

Ethan smiled. "I like that. I'm going to steal it."

"It's all yours. Go back to V. Behave yourself."

He put his hood up. "No promises. She gets frisky in the mornings."

Her hands were up to her ears like a shot. "La la la la, I can't hear you, Ethan!" When she was done she turned off the light, and he vanished into the ether.

Victoria was up early, eager for breakfast and to get back to her sister by lunch. "Do you mind if you shower alone today?" she asked. "I have a call or two to make."

He feigned a pouty face but agreed. It couldn't be sexy showers all the time.

He showered quickly, dried off, and formulated a plan he'd pondered for a while. He'd have to make some magic to have it happen, but it could be fun for both of them. He walked out of the bathroom, toweling his hair, trying his best to act sexy with another towel barely wrapped around his waist and nothing else on. There was always a hope for some morning fun.

"Hey," he began, "I was thinking, maybe you could come out to my place sometime? I can buy the ticket. It's no big deal. The airline owes me for a lifetime of pain anyway. Maybe for a weekend? I know that's longer than our usual visits, but Seattle is so nice once the sun comes out in late spring, and if it's okay…" He stopped, realizing that she was completely ignoring him, staring at her phone, eyes wide and confused. "Hey, is everything alright?"

No answer. She just looked at the phone, and then up at him.

He was suddenly very self-conscious, in a very human way. "What?" he asked, looking over his body, feeling stupid for walking out like this and being so fucking presumptuous. "Did I say something scary? I'm sorry. I just thought a change of scenery might be…"

"Who are you?" she asked very pointedly. There was no mistaking the question.

He was honestly confused. "What?"

She stood, walking over to him. Her small stature meant nothing. She was now twenty feet tall in his eyes, and he felt very tiny. "Who the fuck are you?"

"I'm... I'm Ethan?" Shit. Double shit. What was happening? *Don't tap the magic, stupid. Figure this out. Be a real human.* "Same as I was last night? Same as I've been my whole life. Why? What's going on?"

She threw her phone at him almost accusatorially, insisting he look at it. He obliged, totally unsure what was happening.

And then he looked at the screen.

Oh fuuuuuuuuuuuuck.

On the screen was a room he knew very well. It was Laurel's. She was sitting up in bed, and a dark, unmistakable figure was standing at the foot of it. He'd know that stupid face anywhere.

It was him.

"What the fuck is this?" he asked, honestly unsure. "Where did you get this?"

She snatched the phone back, slamming it on the complementary hotel desk. "It's last night!" she told him. "I wanted to see how she was doing because she was so bad lately, and I found this!"

Mother fucker... She had said they were monitoring Laurel closer since she'd taken a turn for the worse, including, as she had told him if he'd had half a brain to hear the words for what they were, *'some things she honestly doesn't even know about, but we were afraid if she knew she'd get mad'.*

Things like secret surveillance cameras.

Laurel's family had installed a camera in her room to make sure she was safe or to see if she needed help. Of course she wouldn't want that. Who the fuck would want to know they're being watched all day long just in case they fucking died?! It was morbid! It was fine that they loved her, but the optics were terrible.

That didn't matter now, though. He was already in it up to here. He had taken actual, corporeal form when he visited her. He didn't think anything of it. If someone burst in he could vanish instantly, but his stupid fucking need to be more human had now exposed himself in a way he couldn't possibly escape.

Why? Why were you so fucking stupid? It only would have taken one look! Once quick fucking glance around the room to sense something was wrong. But no, you had to try and grow a fucking heart and act like a normal person and now you have a serious fucking problem on your hands!

"Is that you?" she accosted. "Is that you in my sister's room last night?"

Deflect, stupid. Deflect like you've never deflected before! "I was here, with you. How could I be in two places?"

"A great fucking question!" she shot back, her face turning red. "I was up once or twice, and I'd swear to fucking God you were there with me, but this," she pointed at the phone, her voice slowly taking on hysterics, "I can't answer this!"

"Why do you think it's me?" Why? Why were men like this? *Just be honest, you stupid shit! Do you really think you can out-talk and out-duel her here?*

"Look at it!" She picked it up and pulled it up again. "We've been around each other non-stop for months! Do you think I don't know you? Your body? Your voice? She says your name!" Ah shit, there was audio. Of course there was. "Even your inability to wear color! It's all right there! But do you want to know what really blows my fucking mind?"

He didn't want to know. He really, really didn't.

Despite his wishes, she looked back at the phone and flipped through it, looking for something. He prayed she'd never find what she was looking for. He could have stopped it. He could have bent the ways of the world and deleted it, or maybe even find ways to make her mis-remember it and change details or something, but he didn't. He knew this moment was coming. To his credit, he took it like a man. A stupid, stupid man. For Ethan, it was very on-brand.

She thrust the phone back in his face. "Explain this!" He watched. Laurel was leaning back on the bed as it went down. He could hear their conversation. He knew what was coming.

Sure enough, she turned off the light to go to sleep, instantly turning the video image a pale green. *Screw you, night vision. You used to be cool!*

The quality wasn't perfect, but it was unmistakable. Ethan was standing there, and then like a Star Trek hologram, he faded away into nothing.

Damn. No pretty words or slick talk are going to get me out of that one.

His shoulders slumped. Defeat never looked less sexy than a broken twenty-something realizing everything good in life was about to leave him. He could see it coming like a freight train at the end of a tunnel he couldn't escape, getting closer and closer. He couldn't hug the walls or dive under the wheels. He was going to get hit head-on.

"That's a pretty neat trick!" she accosted him, once more grabbing the phone back. "I would be pretty impressed if I wasn't terrified out of my god damned mind!" She walked away to the other side of the hotel room while Ethan just stood in a towel, all dreams of sexy time long faded. "Talk. What the hell did I just see? Was that you?"

He had spent too long in the role and had been too unlucky in it to bother trying to lie at this point. "Yeah. That's me."

She turned back, her eyes red. "How? How did you slip out of here? How did you get to her? How the hell did you disappear? I can't figure any of this out and I can't tell you how much my brain wants to."

"No, I'll bet you can't. It must be pretty fucking confusing." *Don't condescend or attempt to empathize, you idiot! Look at her! She's hurting and confused! Tell her the truth! Tell her the truth and then prove it to her! You knew this day was coming! You knew and you didn't do sweet fuck all to prepare! You need to fix this. No, here's a harder task: you need to not make this worse!*

Ha, good luck with that. Making things worse was basically Ethan's full-time job at this point. He'd already gone pro. Being Death is about as "worse" as someone could get.

He raised his shoulders again. If he was going to do this, he was going to do this with his back straight and his eyes forward.

For some reason, he had a sudden image of his mother flash into his mind, hunched over the table in the large, empty warehouse she was trapped, her multiple personalities of dedicated mother and certifiable fuck-up battling each other while some giant machine behind her fired blueberry muffins out like clockwork.

She wouldn't stand and face her fate the way he would. This was a skill he had learned all on his own. He was growing. But right now, growing wouldn't help him.

"I'm going to tell you this. After I'm done, you're going to either yell at me or cry in silence, I can't quite tell, but when I'm done, I'm going to ask you to do me a favor."

"It's pretty fucking bold to expect that right now," she glowered at him.

"I know, but it will make what I have to say a lot easier. If our time together has meant anything to you like it has for me, I hope you'll listen."

She crossed her arms, the universal signal during an argument for "this better be good or you're a dead man".

Ha. The joke was on her.

"Two years ago I survived a plane crash. Soap and willpower saved my life when one hundred and thirteen others died. After that, I was confronted by a man, the one I've been referring to as my boss. He offered me a job. An unconventional job. A job I didn't know existed. I've been doing it ever since. Some days I'm great at it. Some days are harder. And some days... well... some days I really should have stayed in bed."

Still no movement from the woman across the room.

"Victoria, you won't believe me when I say this, but I am Death. *The* Death. The Shepard in the Field at the End of the Lane. For all things, and everywhere."

Her eyebrows bent downwards forcefully. He was losing her.

Fuck it, he'd already lost her. She was likely plotting her exit away from this mad man as he spoke.

"I am the first ever living Death. I am Ethan Dessier, and Death is my job. I visited your sister because a mistake I made some time ago had repercussions, and those repercussions have affected her in a way I've never seen, and I've been working with her to see why."

"What the hell did you do to my sister?!" she shouted, her face angrier and in more pain than he'd ever seen before.

He raised his hands in a pointless attempt at a calming motion. "Nothing! At least, not directly. She sees things. Things that have happened to me, in other places, in other worlds. That's what she draws in her book. That's where she gets her ideas. It's from her connection to me."

He was so tempted to prove it. He could snap his fingers and take her anywhere and show her. Or he could just take her to Laurel to back up the story. He could do a million things, but he did none of them. In the state she was in, it would have done more harm than good.

"So," he continued before she had a chance to speak, "before you decide whether or not one of us is crazy, here's my ask: go home. Go home and talk to Laurel. Go home and look in her book. In there, near the front, you'll find two pictures of people. Ones that she drew months and months ago."

Victoria was still red, tears streaking down her face, but she seemed to understand. "I remember. I remember her working on them. Her hands were flying she was so motivated to get them done. I'd never seen her work like that before."

Oh thank God. That made this next part easy. "Right. And you remember when she did that?"

"Yeah, back in September or early October I think. Sometime in the fall."

"Alright. Remember that. Go to her and look at them. Talk to her. She'll tell you the same as me, but I'd rather you hear it from your sister than some guy you've only known for a short time."

"It's not just a short time!" she cried out. "At least it doesn't feel like it! God damn it, Ethan, I don't understand! Death!? Do you get how fucking crazy that sounds?"

"I do. Very much. I was the same way when I heard. That's why I'm not going to do anything weird or creepy or strange or show you some kind of magic trick power that I have. I know it won't do any good. That's what the guy who taught me about it did, and it was not safe either physically or mentally. Don't even ask about fucking caddles!" To her credit, she didn't. It was just a blank expression now. Good. He didn't want to remember them anymore anyway.

"The man who showed me this world basically assaulted me with information, beating me into the ground with the unbelievable. But that worked. It sucked, and it hurt, but it worked. I like you too much. Probably more than too much." The next words choked in his throat. "Probably more than 'like', if I'm being honest, which is why I was afraid of this. I knew it was coming and I was terrified. But here we are, like some ridiculous romcom moment, telegraphed the entire time by my own stupidity, and I still didn't stop it because I just wanted to be human for you, and I wanted you to want the human me, so I ignored it like an idiot. So, please, go. Go home. See what she says. See what she shows you. And if, after all of that, you still don't understand, then so be it. You won't see me again."

Her lip quivered. "Why?" The pain in the word shook him to his absolute core. "Why, Ethan? Or whoever the hell you are? Why?"

There was no answer to that. Not a good one. Not one that would satisfy her. And like a fool, he tried anyway. "Because you are more to me than my stupid job, and if you ever realize how big that statement is, I hope that answer is enough."

She looked at the ground, eyes lost in the patterns of the generic hotel carpeting. "You know that there's no way I can believe you, right? That's the stupidest fucking thing I've ever heard."

"I know. That's why I'm not trying to dazzle you with the unbelievable. It's just too much for someone to take. I can't do that to you."

"Why, because you think you love me? Because you think that I love you?" Ethan didn't think it was possible for words to hurt as much as those ones did. They hadn't mentioned love, but things had been going so naturally that he felt they both knew it was coming, and it didn't scare either of them. That was how he knew it was real, the first time he realized that simple fact: it wasn't if, it was when.

Hearing the word escape her lips as an accusation instead of the proclamation he had wanted so badly simply gutted him like a fish. He had no response to give.

It was for the best. A moment later Victoria walked quickly around him, giving him a wide buffer, hurriedly collected her belongings in her overnight bag, and walked to the door. With her hand on the handle, she looked briefly over her shoulder. He could see the redness and tears still there, but she said nothing. And then she turned back and walked out the door.

Huh. Silently crying. Called it.

CHAPTER 14

It had been days since the confrontation in the hotel. How many days, Ethan couldn't tell. Once Vic left his room, and he took a moment to scream into the void at the top of his lungs like a kid throwing a tantrum, he vanished into the underworld of Death to immerse himself in his work. He didn't cry, though. He was past that. He was so unsurprised it had blown up in his face so spectacularly that laughter at his idiocy was more common.

God damn, did his heart hurt. That ridiculous teenage pain didn't go away. Life really was like high school forever if you let it be.

But how was he supposed to handle this? There was no playbook for being an abstract concept, while also navigating the world of regular human life. It wasn't like he was a criminal or something. What if two people were dating but then one of them said that they were actually Santa Claus in real life, or that in another world they were actually the law of gravity. That was how bonkers it sounded to hear your supposed boyfriend was Death.

Every now and then he'd peek into his reality, mostly to check his phone in the faint, baffling hope that he would see her name pop up declaring that all was forgiven. After the first few days, that probability dropped to near-zero as far as he was concerned.

He did, however, have a number of texts and calls from Arlene. They, to be blunt, were not complimentary. However, for as scathing as they were ("I told u nt 2 fuck up my wedding, u *shit emoji*! Plz plz plz fix this or put it n a good place b4 then!"), they weren't completely incendiary.

Gee, thanks for the help and support, Arlene. The emojis really sold the anger. This was really on her, though. She had to realize he would fuck this up somehow. That was his entire modus operandi at this point in life.

Finally, after a few days of sound and fury, she sent a voicemail that was bordering on sweet. In the haze of the chaos he was purposefully wrapping himself up in, it was a moment of clarity.

"Hey," she sounded almost apologetic. "I get that you're likely ghosting me, but don't... don't get stupid. Don't disappear. I need you. I'm not stupid enough to think that this... whatever it is that you and V had going was a guaranteed thing." The "had" in that sentence burned his ears. "But you're both good people, and I doubt whatever it was that caused this was stupid or small."

Ha. So she didn't know. Victoria hadn't told her that her brother was claiming to be Death incarnate. That was a win, right? He honestly had no idea.

"So," she went on after taking a breath, "things are still moving ahead. I'll be sure not to double book you two in the same room until you work this out. And if you don't..." She stopped. The silence was louder than a jumbo jet in his ears. "... If you don't, know that I still want you there. I need you there, and I know both of you well enough to know that everyone can be grown up about this. For what it's worth, I really liked you two together."

Yeah, so did he.

"So, let me know you're ok. I have one last request of you before the big day, and there are a couple other details we need to work out. Don't disappear. Don't..." he could hear her measuring her next words very carefully, "...Don't beat yourself up. Yeah, I think whatever happened was your fault." Ouch. Accurate, but, like, ouch. "But your fault or not, as humans go, you don't suck."

Ooo, nice callback.

"I *will* talk to you soon, ass."

Fuck. Her and her god damned heart. He was so lucky their

mother hadn't crushed hers like she had his.

He owed her something. The last time he'd disappeared like this she'd risked her professional life to make sure he was okay. He fired a text back.

> **Hey. Sorry. Yeah, I was a shit. No surprise. I promise I'll be civil. No hard feelings on my end. I wish I hadn't fucked it up. I really do. What else do you need from me?**

The message went to "read" almost at once, and those ominous three dots appeared almost as fast.

> **Glad ur alive. Y do u suck so bad?**

> **Genetics.**

> **Fuck off. So about my request: color.**

> **Wah?**

> **Color. Ur job is 2 wear color. Nothing stupid. No lime green. Wow me.**

Ah c'mon, Arlene. Why not ask him to pull the moon from the sky.

> **Seriously?**

> **Yep.**

> **Do you want Mt Everest with that?**

> **Nope. Just color. Be tasteful.**

Jesus. All the infinite powers of the universe at his disposal and he still thought the ask was a stretch. "Fine. Are you taking me shopping like you said?"

Nope! I trust u. We'll talk soon. Luv u, bye!

Love you too, sis.

He hated 'luv'. If you're going to say it, fucking say it!
Three more dots appeared as he was putting the phone away.

**For wat its worth, I think she misses u. Like, n a
gud way.**

That one he just left alone. He did not want to think about it. It
wasn't his call how she felt. When they had parted, he put the ball
firmly in her court, and that return shot had been deafeningly silent.

He went back to work.

Dotty was an absolute wreck, her eyes awash with tears and
confusion.

And the pain. Good God, the pain was horrible.

She had been on her way home from work. A quiet night in the flat
was all she was looking for. A cup of tea. A book or some music. She
didn't have a TV. She never felt the need for one.

And then the sound of something very loud startled her, and the
impact from her left was like nothing she'd ever experienced before.

The crunch as something t-boned her SUV and sent it flying was
otherworldly. Then came the tumbling, rolling through the English
fields surrounding the backroads she took home repeatedly as if it
would never end. Somewhere along the line she had smashed her
head on something, but she had no idea what. She was a marionette
and gravity was pulling the strings.

She hadn't even seen any lights coming. It wasn't even at an intersection. There had been no warning at all.

And then she finally stopped moving, dangling sideways as the seatbelt held her in place. Everything hurt. Literally everything.

She could see the blood falling from her head in a steady stream, and she had enough awareness to know that it was a dangerous amount. That was when the crying began. She just wanted to go home. That hot tea felt so inviting right now. She didn't want to die out here. Not in the rainy dark, alone and bleeding out after some stupid accident.

Footsteps approached her. Was it someone from the other car? They could get help. She still had a chance! There were no streetlights out here, but even in the darkness she could tell they were wearing very dark colors.

Someone peered through the smashed front window, grabbing it with their hands and ripping it from the frame like it was paper. A young man looked at her, the ambient light from the interior and the headlights illuminating him just enough to make out a handsome young face.

"Help… help me, please."

"I will," he said, in a very un-native accent. American maybe? That or Canadian. Hard to say. "I've already called for help. It will be some time, though. Too much time, I'm afraid."

"Can you help me?"

The soft rain covered him, but he radiated a certain warmth. It was almost comforting. "What would you like me to do?"

"Help me down?"

"I can do that. I warn you, it won't tickle." That she had assumed.

She wasn't panicking. He moved with a certain grace and carefulness, his hands using a strength his body didn't give away. Moments later he had her, pain still everywhere, but she was out of the SUV now.

In the darkness she couldn't make out the vehicle that had hit her. "What about the other car? Are they okay?"

The young man held her in his arms. It was comforting. Soothing, even. "There was no other car, Dotty."

The fact that he said her name didn't even register. Her head was too swimmy now. "Then what hit me?"

The young man looked up into the darkness, looking for something. "Well, it appears to be a train car. Or at least a part of one. Looks like it was hauling grain of some kind."

The words confused her. "Train car? There's no tracks out here."

"No," he agreed. "No there is not. It was an accident. It wasn't supposed to be here.

Yeah, no kidding. How had she been hit by a rogue train car?

As if reading her mind, he answered. "It's not from around here. It's from some version of India, if I'm reading the side correctly. Not your India, but one close enough."

His words made no sense. "How…? Is help on the way?"

"Yes," he answered, "but as I said, it will be too little too late. But I'll stay with you."

"Thank you," she answered, genuinely glad he had been here. Wait, why was he here? These roads were empty at this time of night. He surely couldn't have been walking alone. "Who are you? What's your name?"

He looked back at her. Was he crying, or was it the rain? "My name is Ethan, from Chicago. Or Seattle. Or whatever. Ethan from America. Fuck yeah."

Dotty looked up confused. "Why? What are you doing out here? Not that I'm not…" She started coughing. There was absolutely blood in it. She could taste it. "…not grateful," she finished.

"I'm here for you. This is a mistake I made, and I'm here to help you as best I can before the end."

"Mistake? Was it your train?" It was a stupid question, but she didn't know what else to say.

"No, but the big fucking hole in reality that pulled it here and let it hit you sure was. I was just in the area looking after a sheep that met an untimely end in a flooded creek and then *poof*! Train car. Another of my mistakes coming back to haunt me. And haunt you, unfortunately. And for that, I can't tell you how sorry I am."

"Am… am I dying?"

"Yes." No hesitation from him. Straight and to the point. The words were terrifying, but she appreciated his directness. "You are. You are, and you weren't supposed to. It wasn't your time. I'm telling you that knowing what headaches it may cause me, and I guess I'm sorry for that too. But I'm in a bit of a low place right now, and I don't really have the ability to get out of it."

If her arms worked, she would have reached out for him. "You… You are Death." A statement, not a question.

Again, no hesitation. "Yeah. I'm that, too. Not many people call me out on it, though."

Dotty had been raised well. Loving parents. A wonderful older brother who looked after her through her formative years after their parents died (now all were gone, God rest their souls), and she knew sorrow when she saw it. She did not know this young man, but she saw he was hurting. Hurting, and tired, despite being so young.

"This was an accident?"

"Yes," Ethan nodded, water dripping from his head as he did so. "A complete accident. I was trying to stop something terrible. I was trying to save the world. I know you don't know what I mean but…"

She stopped him. "Tsk. Shush. It's alright. I just needed to know. I needed to know you didn't want to hurt me."

"No," he agreed. He was crying now. She could tell. Death was weeping over her, of all people? "I never wanted to hurt anyone. That's a pretty stupid thing for Death to say, isn't it."

"No. It's a smart thing for a person to say. It tells me what I need to know about you, the young man who made a mistake. Does everyone get to speak with you like this when it's their time?"

"No," he answered honestly. "It's something I've been doing recently. Letting my human side show through a bit more. It's not going well."

"Well," Dotty coughed, "I'm thankful you took the time for a boring old lady like me."

"There's nothing wrong with boring, Dotty. Boring is great. It may not change the world, but it can make people happy."

She looked out at the countryside. It was beautiful in the summer. It was shit in the late spring like it was now, but you couldn't pick these things. "Alright, let's get on with it."

"I'm sorry?"

"Death. I'm ready. It's been a good run. I don't even want to know what I'm going into. Just do it."

Ethan looked flustered. "I... uh... well, I don't actually do the taking, per-se. I just kinda... uh... you know, I don't really know how to explain this. Can't say I've ever really been put on the spot like this before. You English and your stiff upper lip just throws me off. Let's just say I clean up the aftermath."

"Oh," she answered, her voice cracking as the blood filled it again. She spit it out. "I'm sorry, that's not very ladylike, is it."

"I promise you I've seen worse. It won't be long now. Can I get you something? Something to help?"

"You're here. As you said, most don't get this treatment, do they."

"No," he agreed. "I felt particularly responsible for you."

"Oh, my dear, that's very kind of you. There is something you could do for me, if you wouldn't mind?"

"Name it."

"Well, forgive this old English woman her stereotypes, but I was very much looking forward to my evening cuppa when I got home. I'm not sure what you can do, but if there's a way..."

Ethan readjusted himself, propping her up with one arm, her head against his chest. "Say no more." A cup, specifically *her* cup, the same dusty rose one as the one in her cupboard, appeared in his other hand. Steam came out the top. The smell hit her and made her smile, even through the stench of mud, petrol, and death.

He held the cup to her lips and she drank. The temperature was just right, the milk was spot on, and the flavor was unmistakable.

She stopped, savoring the taste. "Oh. Oh my dear, that is lovely. Thank you."

"No," he said, his voice obviously cracking now. "No, thank you. I did this to you. I fucked this up. Just another in a long list of things lately."

"Oh bah," she said, "the fact that you stayed tells me what I need to know about you. I'm sorry for your pain." She spoke from the heart, as if something was telling her he needed to hear it. A message she believed, but perhaps wasn't directly just her own. A force and power in words the likes of which she had never felt before.

"Thank you. You don't owe me kindness. You don't owe me shit. Not after this."

She thought back to words her dear father used to tell her, on the nature of true kindness. "We owe each other nothing. We give to each other freely, only because we can. That is how we show we truly care."

In the arms of Death himself, Dotty breathed her last on the wet, dark road a moment later. Death took every bit of the light of her life and placed it exactly in the spectrum of greatness where it belonged with a level of attention and care he still didn't believe was enough for what she had just given him.

And Ethan cried.

He stood off to the side, hidden in the shadows as the ambulance took poor Dotty away.

What was that? What the fuck had just happened? In an English field that now inexplicably had half a train car in it, something that was already baffling the local inspectors as they worked the accident scene, why had a random stranger showed him kindness for such a horrible thing?

It had been Dotty's first time "dying right" and damned if she didn't nail it. No walkouts or The Beneath for her.

Why?

Baffled and heartbroken, he faded into the darkness and went back to work.

CHAPTER 15

He was in Russia the next day, overseeing a tragic but totally natural culling of rodents in a freak snowstorm, when his phone buzzed. Another perk of being ethereal was that he didn't have to pay international roaming on his phone plan. Or for any plan at all. So long as he was here, it just worked.

The name on the text surprised him. It was Laurel.

Hey. Can we talk tonight?

He had stopped in to see her a few times since the break-up with Victoria back in April. Still no word from her sister, though. By now he had accepted that that ship had sailed. He didn't check in with her through the veil. He couldn't take it.

His visits with Laurel were brief. She admitted Vic had come home and confronted her about everything. Laurel admitted it and told her what she knew. She showed her the pictures, just like he hoped she would, but the results had not been glowing acceptance. They had been empty nothingness from Victoria.

"She just stared at the image of you," she had said. "Just stared and then put the book down."

Laurel had then told him that she was thankful for what he'd done for her, and kept doing, but she needed her sister more than ever these days. She had taken a liking to his phrasing from when they first met. "That aperture is getting tighter now." Not a question. "It's coming into focus pretty good."

He had said nothing in reply, and that was answer enough.

"I'd like to see you again before the actual time, but you don't need to check on me anymore. I'll be fine."

It hurt to have someone he considered a friend say that, but he had listened. This text was the first he'd heard from her since then.

"I'll be there," he replied. It wasn't her time yet. He obviously knew that, but it was close. Very close. Too close.

It was still the afternoon in Valparaiso when it was early night in Russia. He just had to kill some time. Time had the amazing ability of going both too fast and too slow when it marched towards something you didn't want to do but knew you had to.

Shortly before one in the morning, he visited Laurel. The lights were off, but he knew she was awake. She was sitting up, waiting for him.

He apparated slowly into one of the desk chairs. Since the incident with the camera, which Laurel had assured him they removed after she got very angry about it, he made a point to stay obfuscated as much as possible, invisible to all but the one he was there to speak with. They weren't going to catch him again.

"Hi Ethan," she said when he fully appeared. "Thanks for coming."

"Of course," he replied. "How are you?"

"Cancer-ridden and lovin' it." Her voice was so much weaker now. "Do you mind if I turn on the light?"

"Not at all. It's your bedroom."

The light came on. It was a softer light than it had been. Her family had apparently reduced the wattage. "New light," she said, looking at his face. "The old one was hurting my eyes."

Laurel looked every bit as sick and weak as she sounded now. It was amazing she was even holding on, but she was.

"Sorry if I'm not much to look at," she said softly, clearly self-conscious.

"Oh, whatever. You know who I am. You're actually doing

surprisingly well. It's good to see you."

"You liar. But thanks. I'm trying." He could see that. Her will was strong. "I saw there was another rip yesterday. A nasty one. When I saw it I felt you may want to talk about it."

The pain of the death of the innocent Dotty caused him to wince. It had only been a few hours, or had been a billion lifetimes, but it was still fresh in his mind. "Yeah. Not my finest moment."

"Oh I don't know," she answered. "That old lady seemed to appreciate you."

Ugh. Laurel and her insights into his mind. "I guess. I still feel pretty shitty about that, though."

Laurel looked at him thoughtfully. "I can imagine, but she was right. It was an accident."

"An accident indirectly caused by a major mistake I made. Whether it's one life or a billion, every life I lose because of what I did hurts."

Laurel reached over and took her drawing book from the bedside table. Her movements were labored and looked uncomfortable, but she waved him off when he offered to help. She flipped through the pages and came to the last one. The book was almost full. She had laboriously continued drawing what she had seen him go through. She said it made her feel better, and gave her mind something to focus on.

"I wanted to show you my latest one." She placed her fingers on something he couldn't see and then turned it around. "I think it may be my masterpiece."

The image took Ethan's breath away.

On the page, in her now-unmistakable style, was the most beautiful, heartbreaking, human image Ethan had ever seen. He never had a taste for art, but as they say, he knew what he liked. It was him, his face obscured and looking down, dressed in his regular black. He was knelt on the ground, the broken lines of an accident behind him. In his arms was the woman known as Dotty. He never knew he could look so strong. He cradled her in his arms while she held the teacup. It was the cup itself that radiated. The image was all grays and dark blues of the night and rain, but the cup was glowing in dusty rose, drawing the eye to it. A beacon of light in a very dark time.

Although he didn't cry, he could feel his cheeks flush as he leaned forward and took the book, his eyes going over the page, memorizing every line and detail.

"This is the most beautiful thing I think I've ever seen," Ethan said honestly, his voice hitching.

"Well, don't let my sister hear you say that."

Ethan shook off her words. He couldn't think about Victoria right now. That was too much pain to bear. "I mean it. It's amazing. The light. The color. The emotion. Everything. It's... I just... I've got nothin', Laurel. It's amazing."

"Thank you. I'm pretty proud of it."

"You should be," he stifled a slight sniffle. "Though I'm sorry you had to see it."

"I'm not. I couldn't be happier."

He looked at her. The moisture in his eyes twinkled in the faint light.

"It's why I wanted to see you," she said. "I wanted to tell you what I saw."

He swallowed. It was like a rock in his throat. "Tell me what you saw."

She sat up, suddenly showing more strength than a moment before. "This is the most human thing I've ever seen, Ethan. You may be Death, whatever the hell that means, but this isn't a picture of Death, this is a picture of you. This is Ethan Dessier, the human being, showing kindness. Showing unimaginable amounts of humility and compassion in the face of tragedy. I want you to see that as well."

He looked back at the image. He saw it. At least, he thought he did. He would never forget this picture. This moment in his life.

Even still, in the beauty of it, and all the feelings it summoned inside of him, Ethan had to be Ethan. Being Ethan was the only way he knew how to deal with emotions this big.

"You know," he said, sniffling slightly, "Dotty never held the cup. I held it for her."

"Are you critiquing my work? Call it artistic license. I thought this looked more realistic. More like the moment being what it actually was."

"Well," he ran his hand under his nose, "I'm just saying, it's beautiful, but it's factually inaccurate."

She smiled at him. "You are such an asshole."

He laughed back, handing the book over to her again. "I never claimed otherwise."

"No, that's for damn sure."

The voice came from behind him, startling him and causing him to jump from the chair. Once again the movies lied. He wasn't ready for a fight. He was ready to piss himself.

Victoria stood by the closet door. She had been hiding inside it. Likely listening to the entire conversation.

You dumb fuck! You didn't look around again! Jesus Christ, you're bad at this!

After the removal of the camera and his making himself invisible to prying eyes, he thought he was safe.

"Sorry," Vic said, somewhat amused at his reaction, "I didn't want to scare you. No, wait, that's a lie. Yes I did. I wanted to see if I could."

Ethan looked from her to Laurel, who was smiling at him. It wasn't a happy smile, but an amused one. One that said he deserved that.

With his heart returning to normal rhythm, Ethan relaxed. "That's fair. It's good to see you, Vic."

"You too, Ethan." She walked softly and slowly to the other side of Laurel's bed, taking her sister's frail hand and looking at her. "She called me in here last night. Told me she wanted me to see something." She ran her hand over the book that Laurel had returned to the table. "I agree with what you said." She looked into his eyes and his heart sank. He was helpless here in front of her, laid completely bare. "This is the most beautiful thing I think I've ever seen."

The pain of the cause was still fresh. "Dotty didn't deserve it," he said, his voice still fluctuating. "She was never going to change the world, but she was a good woman. A woman who is dead now because of a mistake I made." He looked at Victoria, thankful not to see malice in her eyes but compassion, and more than a little confusion. "Look, I know this doesn't mean shit to you, but I swear I never meant for this to happen. And I mean, like, all of it. Everything that's fucking up your head and mine right now." He looked at Laurel. "And I never meant for you to see it. I never meant for you to feel my pain. Not when you have enough shit to deal with it."

Laurel shrugged. "Actually, it's been a fantastic distraction. Like it or not, I wouldn't have it any other way."

Victoria released her sister's hand and began to walk around the end of the bed, her eyes on Ethan as she moved. "Who are you?" she asked.

He remembered the last time she asked this question, while he foolishly held a towel around his waist. This wasn't like that. That was fear. This sounded like genuine curiosity.

"I'm Ethan Dessier," he answered. He wanted to add more but didn't.

She kept walking. "Is that all?"

Ethan stood firm, even though her eyes on him made his legs shake.

"It's all that matters."

She stood in front of him now, barely outside arm's reach.

"Show me."

The words rang in his ears like church bells.

"What do you mean?" he asked. He wasn't sure he knew what she was asking. He couldn't assume anything.

"Are you also Death?" she asked.

He braced himself. "I am."

A quick head nod. "Alright. Then show me."

He still wasn't sure what she was asking. "I'm sorry, it's been a crazy day, so I'm going to be a dick and ask for specifics. Show you what?"

Her eyes were clearly red, even in the poor lighting. She was fighting so many emotions, but he let her be for now. He could wait. He could have the patience for a moment like this. He wasn't just asking her to accept him. He was asking her to redefine her faith, her entire structure of beliefs, everything she thought she knew about the world, all just for him. It was not a small ask. Eventually, she built up the courage she felt she needed. "Ethan," his name on her lips again. Clear. Real. Substantiative. "It's time for you to dazzle me with the unbelievable."

CHAPTER 16

When the previous Death had confronted him, appearing randomly in his quiet loft apartment and making strange Canadian coffee and using their intense squirrel-energy to captivate Ethan two years previous, Ethan had thought it was all bullshit, obviously.

Death seemed to take that personally, and proceeded to randomly throw Ethan into new, strange worlds in an effort to get the point about who and what he was across to Ethan in the fastest and most "baseball bat to the side of the head" manner he possibly could.

In the end it had worked, but Ethan fought against it the entire time. It was amazing, but it was terrifying.

When she finished speaking the words, and he saw the conviction in her red eyes, Ethan swore that he couldn't do that to her. Not to someone he…

He caught himself. *Oh no you don't, you son of a bitch. You've gotta crawl before you walk off the earth.*

Thankfully, that thought guided his next move expertly.

He reached his hand out, asking silently for hers in return.

She could have tortured him by refusing, or even worse, just doing nothing, but instead she took his hand without hesitation.

Sweet Jesus, did he miss the feel of her touch.

Shake it off, lover boy. Focus up.

Before he did anything abrupt, he looked at Laurel. "Permission to escort your sister away for a moment?"

Laurel smiled. "Of course. I'm tired anyway. Don't stay up late."

Victoria looked at them both with wonder, but also appreciation. A part of her was thankful Laurel had someone like Ethan near the end. Laurel had her friends, sure, but they had come and gone. People who knew her when she was healthy and vibrant had difficulty dealing with her as she faded away. Vic didn't blame them, but she didn't forgive them either. In Ethan, it seemed she had a friend who didn't care. A friend that made her feel happy. That made Laurel feel safe, despite her anger and confusion at what he had done.

Ethan nodded in agreement and looked at Vic. "I've never done this before. Not to someone else anyway."

"Just don't let me fall."

He had no idea what she was referring to, what image of what was about to happen she had in her head, but little did she know the statement was incredibly apt for where he was planning on taking her first.

A moment later they disappeared from Laurel's bedside without a sound.

Laurel only smiled.

Victoria wasn't sure what happened. She was in Laurel's room, holding Ethan's hand (God how she missed his hands), and the next the room was fading away around her and she was in darkness.

When the light started returning around her, she had difficulty determining what she was looking at.

There was a large, red light that formed behind her, and although the sky was dark and full of stars, it felt like daytime. Her feet touched down on a coarse walkway, but a quick squeeze confirmed that Ethan was still there with her. He was as good as his word.

When they had completely reappeared, she released his hand tentatively and looked around. Stars and planets drifted through the black, nebulae swirled, and comets pulsed and shot across the sky. The red light behind her was a massive star, so huge it looked like it would roast them, but she felt fine.

It looked like they were in a park of some kind, with grassy patches and slides and…

No, it wasn't just a park, it was a waterpark, only the pools were empty and dry. That was the coarseness she was walking on, the gritty sandpaper-like ground that waterparks kept everywhere to help people keep their grip when wet.

Actually, now that she recovered from the arrival and was able to actually grasp what she was looking at as a whole, she was positive it looked familiar.

She looked at Ethan, confused. He just stood, allowing her the moment to understand. A moment he himself was never given. He had been bashed in the head, literally and figuratively. For her, he was going to guide her as if floating on a cloud.

"Is this… Mystic Waters? Up in Des Plains?" she asked.

Ethan smiled. "It sure is, or at least, a vision of it. When we were younger, Arlene and I came here with our mom. We both agreed that it was the best time the three of us ever had as a family." Ethan started to look around, parts of his mind remembering that day and the good feelings it gave him.

"Years later," he continued, "that memory would be ruined. Stripped of everything that made it special to my sister and me. I come here when I need to remember the good and the bad. Or when I need to just scream into the void. I figured it was as good a place as any to start with helping you see."

Victoria listened, but didn't understand. She was, however, very startled and impressed with what she was seeing. It was beautiful. "What does this have to do with death?"

Ethan raised his eyebrows. "Ah, right, well, and stay with me here because explaining it isn't easy and I'm scared as fuck: nothing. Well, not really. Death as an action is just death. This is the result." He gestured to the vast expanse beyond. "All of this is a representation of something beyond life. It is a collection of everything, focused for your eyes to see, just as it was mine two years ago. Stars surrounded by hundreds of planets. Galaxies with billions of stars with those planets. Great celestial clusters with trillions of galaxies with billions of stars surrounded by... you get the idea. It's all here, laid out like a shitty planetarium display."

Victoria was overwhelmed, but got the idea. "And you... you control all of this? As Death?" God that felt weird to say.

Ethan shook his head. "No. This exists without me. Death is not an action. It's a job. I'm the universe's biggest, and forgive my pride, most important janitor, cleaning up the shop."

She was still confused. "Look," he continued, "I can't hit you with the glory of the everything, the essence of all life everywhere, because it's just so much for a person's mind to understand, but let me put it this way. When something dies, it splits. It shatters into these glorious little... Idunno, lights, I guess? Like, atoms, or quarks or muons or whatever. I'm no physicist and I'm sure as hell not going to be able to explain this to an engineer. But those things, those lights and bits, they have a place out there." He pointed to the space beyond. "Somewhere in a distant galaxy, near a distant star, on a distant planet, is a new, dawning, beautiful, microscopic, miniscule life forming. When all the pieces are together, its life begins. I take those lights, those atoms, from where they leave their world, and place them where they belong, out there, in the infinite, where they wait to become something else. Something equally amazing."

"What about Laurel?" Victoria asked right away. She either understood the scope of what he was saying or she was ignoring it. Either way she was coming to her own realization of the world. "Will you kill her?"

"Cancer will kill her."

"Then you can kill the cancer."

A reasonable, if not flawed, step in logic. "I can't. Nature is going to do its thing. Someone or something will die and I can't stop it. It's not my job."

"But you said it yourself, you're Death!"

Ethan wondered if that was what he sounded like two years ago.

"I am, but humans as a people misunderstood what death is. It's not the act of losing your life, it's the act of cleaning up where the parts of that life go. The loss of life is just a natural thing, unstoppable and forever, for all its tragedy and beauty. When that life ends, Death gets to work. Much like my real life, Death is always just one step behind."

Victoria looked at Ethan, measuring the truth in his words, trying to understand the scope. "Are you working right now? Out there?" She motioned to the space around them.

Jeez, how was this punch going to land. "Yep. I am Death. I am everywhere, always."

"How?"

"Uhhh… Well, it's kinda hard to explain if you're not actually Death…"

"Try. How can you be everywhere and be here at the same time?"

Ethan wracked his brain for a moment. "Think of it like a house of mirrors. Millions of reflections bouncing around everywhere. All of them are you, but only one of them is the real you. I am in that house of mirrors, only all of them are real. All of them are me. When I want to, I can become one of them. The rest are still out there, doing their job, but I am me. And this, this here," he indicated himself, "this is me. This is Ethan. I told you I am the first living Death. It's a long story that I'd love to tell you, but I want to make this perfectly clear: this is me. With you, it's always been me."

"Except when you slipped out to visit my sister."

Danger, danger! Step lightly, shit head. "Well, you were asleep at the time…" *What? No! Why does my human brain have to control my mouth words!* "… Alright, you're right. But it's a big job, as I'm sure you can appreciate. And what was happening with her was something I've never experienced before."

An accusing look, but not an angry one. "The rips," she said.

"Yeah, those. The pictures she draws are images of them. She has one inside her, tiny and protected by the light of her life. It will be there until the end."

"Yeah, she tried to explain that. It still doesn't make sense. Do you know why it happened to her?"

Ethan shook his head. "No. I'm not sure I'll ever know. I've been trying to find out, but she's running out of time."

The words hit Victoria and she turned sharply, as if the action would make the words go away.

"She says it's fate. Fate that connected you two, to help her get through this cancer bullshit, and maybe help you along the way somehow," Vic whispered. She was crying.

"I know she does. Which is fine. I don't believe in fate. I wanted to find a proper answer. I've failed."

"Death can fail?"

"Ha! This one can. Multiple times. Often epically."

She looked back. "That seems unlikely."

"That's what I thought!" Ethan exclaimed. "I thought 'hey, I'm Death and I have all these powers, I can fix anything!' But I couldn't! I tried to, but I fucked it up. I fucked it up and caused a bigger problem and now I have to fix it. And it's exhausting, Vic, it really is. It's just..." He slumped. "I'm tired. I'm trying to fix it, to make the rips and tears go away, but they're getting worse."

She looked back at him fully, curiosity in her eyes. "What happens then?"

He would never in a billion years expose her to the horror that was the Nothingness without warning. The vast, formless emptiness that would take over if he failed, but he did think he could show her what he was faced with gradually.

God, you better be right about this, or you'll fucking blow it with her forever.

He pointed to the space beyond, and with a motion, everything disappeared. Eventually even the platform they were standing on faded from existence.

To Victoria, it felt like the drop of a roller coaster, and once everything disappeared she couldn't get her bearings at all. Just falling and drifting in inky black.

And then, the falling sensation stopped, and she felt weightless, tumbling through unknowable darkness without a tether. Floating. Helpless.

"This is what happens," Ethan's voice said, filling the void. He really hoped it wasn't too loud or too melodramatic. "Everything is consumed by nothing. This is the balance I keep. This is the job of Death."

She heard the words, but had difficulty processing them in her current situation. "Please," she pleaded, "please put me down."

"Of course," Ethan said, now appearing right beside her, stopping her rotation. "Any requests on where to go? What can I show you? I'm not great at this, but I want to help. What don't you get? What *do* you get? What can help this?"

She grabbed him with both hands, afraid she would fall, but not sure *where* she would fall. "You said it was a mistake that made these rips? Like the one inside Laurel?"

Ah shit. Shit shit shit. He knew exactly where this was going. He knew it, and walked right into it. "Yes. The mistake was why I was hired. It's why I have the job. Death is chosen based on a specific task that needs to be done. This was mine."

Don't say it. Please, don't make me relive it. Please god, don't let her say...

"Show me."

Fuck.

There was no helping it. He was in for a penny and pound now. He desperately wanted this woman back in his life, but not like before, with subterfuge and half-truths. Honesty and truth had to be the course he took. No more fear. No fear of hurting. No fear of what might be.

The plane crash was the most critical moment in his life, but then came the confrontation with the ghost of his mother in the Beneath.

But then, blowing them all away, was the Him.

Ugh, just the thought of him makes me want to fucking vomit.

He knew the best place for this part, though. He had thought about it a million times just on his own. Moments later the two were on a beach, with a forest nearby. It wasn't warm and tropical, but it wasn't cold either.

"Where are we?" she asked.

"An island."

"Yeah, thank you. An island where?"

Jeez, how to explain this.

"Remember about the house of mirrors?" She nodded. "Well, this is a world in a reflection." He had to step carefully. From what they'd spoken of, she wasn't terribly spiritual, but he was still dancing very close to the line of "massive religious experience", and as he'd been told before, he had two left feet. "You with me?" She looked around, said nothing, and then nodded. He didn't need to explain that some worlds were comprised entirely of light, or that in some places time flowed like either pitch or lighting. Baby steps. "Ok, great, then this will be easier. So, we are on an island in another of those worlds. We've gone through a few layers of mirrors."

Oh, you are so smooth and elegant. You should write greeting cards!

"Anyway, in this one, there was a man. A man I was going to be hired to monitor. The great minds of the universe told the specter of Death that this guy was going to really fuck things up, and after much deliberation, I was the thing chosen as the best option to stop him, so they tried to recruit me."

"What happened?"

Ethan shrugged. "I lived."

Realization on her face. "The plane crash."

"Yep. Somehow, through a fluke of luck and willpower, I survived. For the first time since the birth of time itself, someone said 'no', and that someone was me.

"I had just buried my mother and started out on my own. I didn't want to die, and I also didn't want this fucking job, but I was…" *'Job raped'* he believed was the term Death had used, but that wouldn't do here. "…persuaded to take it after seeing how important it was, but a part of the deal was that I got to do it on my own terms. So when all was said and done, I agreed to become a living Death. The first and only one. I age. I have a life. I feel things." He looked at her longingly. "Jesus Christ, do I feel things…"

He snapped out of it, desperate not to look too cringe. He stepped through the sand on the beach. "In this place, on this island, a man, my target, was born. He grew up and became powerful and had a stupid fucking name like something from a comic book. Not important. He lived long and became incredibly powerful, dodging death more than anyone ever had. Not like I did, with willpower and stubbornness, but by simply not seeing it when it could happen. Life, all life everywhere, needs to 'die right', and accept when it's their moment to leave. Their life goes on until it doesn't. It's confusing, I know, but when it was supposed to be my time, Death twisted worlds and reality to force me to accept that death. One hundred and thirteen people did. I did not. This man-god douchebag and I had that in common, but for different reasons. Anyway, eventually, he finally lost a fight, defeated after hundreds of years like some kind of Marvel or Game of Thrones character. It was all very dramatic and I may tell you that story if you want. Anyway, he lost, and he died."

She just watched him, waiting for more. Waiting for the reason her sister could see through reality. He was terrible at telling stories.

He caught her insistent look. "So there he sat, beaten, and I knew that if he died it would cause some more of those rips and whatever. He was too powerful. I couldn't just let him die. He tried to pick his own time of death, also a no-no. He thought after all this time that Death would just take him when he told Death he was ready. He had no idea the problems it would cause if I let that happen."

"Did you save him?"

Ethan looked out to sea. He hated this part. "I forced him to live."

Confusion on her face. "Seems counter-intuitive for Death."

"Yeah, that's what he thought. So he sat there waiting to die while I tried my fucking damndest to convince him to help me fix the problems. He tricked me. He looked like he stewed on it, but then he forced my hand, taking billions of innocent lives with him. Powerful lives. It overloaded me. I couldn't keep up. Who knew Death had limits, right? I sure as shit didn't. And then the rips exploded in frequency because I couldn't keep up with the demand that much power and life being snuffed out at one time created.

"I wanted to help him. To help the world." He remembered the guy's face. Hated it so much. "Help all worlds. It was why I was hired. I figured I couldn't lose. Why would the universe be wrong in picking me? I allowed myself to have a small drop of confidence and it blew up in my fucking face. And then rips became tears, and realities invaded other realities, and things started dying before they were supposed to and without preparation, and it's been downhill ever since. I wanted to save the world. Save life. But I couldn't reason with him. Couldn't bargain. It was a force of nature I couldn't stop."

He stepped over to her, hoping any of this made sense. Hoping he hadn't lost her. "So I have to fix them. I have to make this right. And I don't know when I can leave the job. Maybe forever. Maybe tomorrow. I'm a shopping bag in a dust devil just wanting to touch down."

She came closer to him. "That doesn't seem fair."

He laughed. "Believe me, I've been all over the fabric of space and time, death and life, through multiple universes. At no point have I seen where the promised fairness of life is written. And if it *is* out there, it sure as shit is written in pencil."

Silence for a time. Who knew what she was thinking about.

"So," she said eventually, "you are Death, and you are also Ethan... and you thought you could *reason* with someone instead of just letting them die? *You* did? Like, *Ethan*? You met a man-god force of nature, whatever, and you thought you had the charm to talk your way out?"

"Okay, well, when you put it like that it seems stupid," he agreed. He'd thought about that a million times before. Why did Ethan Dessier think he could out-reason someone? Man, he must have been feeling cocky that day. "But yeah, that was my master plan. Don't blame me! It was the universe than gave me the fuckin' job."

She slowly, cautiously took his hand, standing beside him as they both looked out to sea. "You can go anywhere? Do anything? See anyone? Make anything?"

"There are some limits, and that settlement money is mine fair and square, so I use that a lot because fuck them, but yes, basically."

She squeezed his hand, and the action literally weakened his knees. He had no idea that was a real thing.

"And you can't spare my sister?"

Ugh. The heartbreak in the words. "She's not mine to spare. Nature does what it does. My mistakes caused unnatural death and plenty of it, but cancer is just cancer. Laurel knows this. I've helped her understand as best I can. She'll fight until the very end, but the cancer will win. Death is incredibly personal. A person needs to accept it, and then the process begins, and I just come in to clean things up. Her window is narrowing. It is coming and it is unstoppable. I'm sorry."

"Thank you for doing that for her," Victoria said. "For helping her through it. For trying to reason with her and help her accept it."

He sighed. "Her visions are my mistake. I fix my mistakes. I'll make new ones, but I'll fix those too."

"That may be the manliest thing you've ever said."

Ha. Ethan was not manly. Far from it. "Maybe. I had a brief thing when I was little when I thought lumberjacks were cool. I may have said something awesome then, but I can't remember."

"Ha, I wish I had seen that. If you wanted to give that a try again, I wouldn't argue."

The subtext in her words wasn't missed. It was a light of hope, but he wasn't stupid enough to hope. But he could hope to hope, maybe?

"Ethan, this is a lot."

"No shit. And this is just a sample. It's the single flake on the top of the iceberg. And the iceberg is on an asteroid. And the asteroid is crashing into the Antarctic, but thank you for listening."

Her voice went quiet, almost drowned out by the waves. "When I saw that drawing, when Laurel called me in to see it, I had to talk to you again."

"That was not my finest moment. That woman didn't deserve to die."

"No, she didn't, but I disagree about your finest moment. I think that was the most human I've seen you. It was that humanity that made me want to reach out. You are not a monster."

Her innocence to the things he'd done was refreshing. "Halloween would disagree. A lot of kids out there dressed like me."

"Hey, yeah, do you actually have a scythe? That's the thing, right?"

He shook his head. "Fuck no. Can you imagine me with a scythe? I'd look ridiculous."

More silence. He could feel the thoughts churning in her head, but he left it alone. People needed to make their own decisions. He'd just explained how interfering and trying to persuade someone had possibly doomed all of existence.

"What happens when we die? Like, to the person, not the clean-up you have afterwards," she asked eventually.

It was a massive question, but an understandable one. "It's hard to explain."

"Can you show me? I need to know Laurel will be alright."

Jeez, there was so much more to it than that. "When I was shown exactly what it was, it overloaded my head and I was passed out in a hospital for two days. I still haven't really recovered. There's a dark side to it. A terrible side." He thought of the real Nothing, and the Beneath. Did he explain that?

She turned to face him. He looked down, terrified. God, how he missed her eyes.

"I trust you."

CHAPTER 17

He stood in the hotel room, looking over himself in the stupid mirror, unsure exactly what he was seeing in the reflection. It was so unnatural. So strange. So not him.

But, in another way, he loved it. It was a bizarre combination of everything he hated about himself, and everything he… well, loved was a strong word… Liked? Tolerated? Sure, tolerated about himself.

He got on the elevator and entered the lobby, strutting with pride as he moved. One side of him felt like an absolute tool, but the other was legitimately proud he pulled it off. He had never had much of a reason to strut before, and it felt amazing.

Ethan had crafted the perfect ensemble, completely without the help of Arlene or anyone else. The pants were black, but the shiny new Doc Martens matched the sharp-cut blazer he wore: dusty rose.

The coat itself was floral with black trimming, and the pattern adorning it was suspiciously similar to that of a good woman's teacup that he'd met a few months prior. He'd even "found" sunglasses that matched.

I hope you're with me today, Dotty.

He was going to meet everyone at the venue. He had a lot to think about this morning, but he'd had plenty of time to go over his mistakes in his head in the days and weeks and months leading to this day. Today wasn't the day for his mistakes to take over his mind. Today belonged to someone better.

He stepped out to the entrance and waited for the valet to bring his car around after he'd called ahead from the room. A moment later Ethan walked around to the driver door of the '67 Mustang Cobra, a treat for himself when he concocted this plan. Its paint job matched his suit and shoes to the letter. The Cobra never actually came in this color, but he couldn't help but twist the rules of nature today. He was feeling feisty. He figured the limo full of doves would be wasted anyway.

He rolled through the streets of Chicago on a beautiful summer Saturday, windows open, actually enjoying the looks he got along the way. He didn't like attention at the best of times, but his heart was full today and he wanted to let it show.

He made it to the restaurant, feeling a bit like Jerry Lewis and a bit like James Bond. *I guess that's the duality of man I hear about so often.*

The wedding party had custom parking spots in the lot and he put the Cobra in the one designated for him. He had never felt as cool in his life as he did when he stepped out of that beast. Is this what being popular felt like? Maybe he'd given the jocks and douchebags in high school a hard time. This was addictive as fuck.

He knew she was in there somewhere and his heart skipped. It couldn't be helped. He had to get over his boyhood fears and commit to this, for his sister. He couldn't worry about what else was going on in his life. Those were problems for another day.

He had been instructed to enter the back door, go through the kitchen, and into an adjacent sitting room where the bride and her entourage were waiting after spending a night together in a nearby hotel's penthouse.

The kitchen was bustling, prepping the appetizers and finger foods for the modest attendees. It smelled fantastic. He had been present for the death of each of the shrimps, cows, and even fruits and vegetables on each of the plates, but that was a hazard of the job. Nature gonna nature and all that. Besides, at least one of the shrimps was certifiably evil. He hoped he could eat that one first.

And that *perk* of the job.

The flustered wedding planner found him and hurried him to the sitting room. "You're late," she chuffed.

"And you're a cliché," he fired back. "I'm five minutes early."

"If you're not ten minutes early on a wedding day, you're late," she said, ignoring his dig. Whatever. Not his problem. Everyone had a job to do.

She brought him to the door and he held his breath as it opened.

Inside, Arlene was standing with her back turned, a small crowd around her. For a low-level wedding, it sure had the bluster of a full-scale one. Someone pointed to him, telling her he'd arrived.

His sister turned to greet him. Even he had to admit she looked stunning. The dress choice was absolutely the right one. Score one for the brother's keen eye, he supposed. Instead of greeting him, she thrust her hands on her hips and looked him up and down. He had agreed to wear color, but never said what, how, or how much it would be.

Screw it. He felt like a million dollars. He struck a pose and spun around, letting her drink it all in.

Her eyebrow raised. "Dusty rose?"

"Fuck yeah dusty rose. You got a problem with it?"

She looked him over again. "The shoes are a bit much."

"The shoes make the outfit. Without them I'd look like shit."

He never looked around the room. He didn't want to see if Victoria was in it. He wasn't ready for that. He just focused on Arlene.

Finally, thankfully, she smiled wide at him. "I love it. Great job."

Exhalation. It was a gamble and it paid off. "I aim to please."

"No, you got lucky. If this was a big fancy wedding, I'd have you tarred and thrown out of the church."

"Ha! Like they'd ever let either one of us in a church!"

They both laughed, and he gave her a hug. "You look great," he admitted. "Very little to complain about. Mostly just nitpicky things I'll tell you about later when it's too late."

"Thanks. Strangely enough, so do you. Seven out of ten. Maybe six and a half because of the shoes."

The Dessier siblings: united in backhanded compliments and

sarcasm.

They released the embrace and the planner went back to work, directing things and just generally being a pain in the ass. Ethan sheepishly looked around the room. With no drink in hand and no job to do, he was starting to feel in the way.

She wasn't here. That made him nervous.

Arlene caught his looks. "She's around. Checking stuff out front. Making sure the boys are behaving themselves. I figured it best to keep her away, and she agreed."

"Thanks, Arlene. But I'll behave myself. I promise."

"Yeah, like you promised to wear color. That hardly qualifies. You should have let me take you shopping."

He did his job and stayed out of the way, watching the crowd. The other two bridesmaids were helping and giggling and enjoying the moment. Each wearing a dress of their own choosing in some muted accent color, giving nothing away about what to expect when he eventually found Vic.

Eventually the time came, and the planner hurried Rachelle and Tara to meet Victoria out there somewhere and walk in with the groomsmen. It was just the two of them in the staging room for now.

"The eighty percent ends after today, you know," Ethan deadpanned to break the silence.

"Ha, you think that was eighty? It seems like you cranked it up to four hundred and twelve on occasion."

He smirked. "I didn't say it would be a constant eighty. Eighty was the average. You should have been more specific with your demands. Like, say 'no more than eighty'. Frankly, it was a flaw in the verbal contract you need to own."

More silence for a moment. "Thanks for being here," she said at last.

Keep it under eighty from here on out, Ethan. "Thanks for having me, Arlene. This is the one, right? Matthew is a good guy?"

"Yeah. He's a great guy."

That made Ethan feel better. "Good. I'm glad you found one. It couldn't have been easy. Love is fucking hard."

"It wasn't so bad," she replied. "I just looked for whoever was the complete opposite of you. Then I knew they'd be a winner." He took her hand, ready to lead. "Keep the sunglasses on. They fuckin' rock."

He was happy to oblige.

The door opened into the restaurant. Tables had been pulled away and seats arranged like a proper wedding, all to be moved aside later as the evening went on. Despite claiming to be low-key, it could not have been cheap to buy this place out on a summer Saturday. The upper-middle class at play.

All eyes turned to them, the rest of the wedding party at the front of the room already. His eyes found Victoria at once. No force in the universe could have stopped them.

He swore his heart actually stopped.

She was gorgeous, dressed in a stunning dress that accented her figure as if crafted by Vera Wang herself.

It was a beautiful dusty rose.

How? How did she know?

Whatever. Deal with it later. Focus on your sister. One foot in front of the other right now.

Matthew stepped forward as they got closer, camera flashes from every phone in the room popping like sparklers. Ethan knew his role and went to meet him.

This guy seemed alright. He'd have to do, Ethan supposed.

He took Matthew's hand and shook firmly, and pulled him in for a hug. "She is the only family I have," he told him. "You better look after her with everything you've got. Every ounce of your being better be dedicated to making her happy from this moment forward."

Matthew nodded. "I will, Ethan. You have my word."

"Good," Ethan followed up, "because if you don't, I will fucking kill you. Believe me. I know a guy."

Matthew laughed awkwardly and agreed.

He likely thought Ethan was kidding.

He handed his sister over to this incredibly boring, handsome man, and took his seat in the front row. All of that bluster, all of that time talking and going through things with Arlene, and just like that his job was done.

Well, as much as he hated it, there were a few more things. But for the most part, it was much ado about nothing. A pointless ceremony. Just pageantry and pomp. Things he hated.

Today Death could find a place for them. Only today, though. Tomorrow it was back to mocking and vitriol.

The Justice of the Peace, a sharp-dressed older woman with just the right level of volume and enunciation, clearly honed after years in the craft, led the congregation through the motions. All while Ethan stole looks from behind his glasses at Victoria.

He never once saw her look at him, and it made his heart ache.

Why did someone have this kind of power over him? It wasn't even fair, really. He could control space and time. One woman shouldn't have this hold.

Yet here they were.

The ceremony ended almost as soon as it began. *God bless civil unions*, thought Ethan. After that, the wedding party was ushered into an awaiting limo-van. Ethan was expected to be around for at least a few pictures and agreed to drive separately to meet them there so he could come back when his small part was done. Hence his need for something more than a boring black sedan.

He wished he could have seen his sister's face when the Mustang pulled out behind them, engine roaring and drawing eyes as he pumped the gas every time they stopped or slowed down. He was having the time of his life. He figured this was pushing eighty percent, but only just. Every wedding day needs a story to tell the kids in the future. "And then your asshole uncle pulled out in a pink Mustang. *Pink!* What a dick."

Pictures were at a local park near the lake. Nothing crazy. Everyone agreed they wanted to get back, eat, drink, and get to the only part of the wedding that anyone really remembers and enjoys anyway. Ethan did, however, allow a moment after the van stopped to let the guys go over his ride with a fine-tooth comb, firing off questions he had no answer to since he was never a gearhead of any kind. Boys will be boys.

While they drooled over classic American steel, and while Arlene glowered at him for stealing her newly minted husband mere moments after they said their vows, Victoria finally looked at him through the crowd.

Did she smile? He swore to god she smiled. He could just walk over to her, but he held back. It wasn't his place. Not here. Not now.

Yeah, that was a smile.

A few pictures later (including a couple on the car, after Matthew practically begged for it), and another of Ethan's jobs were done. He hugged his sister ("I'm going to murder you, you prick," she whispered lovingly) and headed back to the venue where he spoke to random strangers about nothing of importance and didn't necessarily hate it.

He had one more job to do.

Dinner was delicious, but he expected that. He didn't have much of a palette, but much like art, he knew what he liked. He made casual conversation with his tablemates, his heart in his throat as the meal wound down.

Death was not a public speaker.

"And now," said the MC, a young man who Ethan believed was Matthew's relative from god-knew-where, "with a toast to the Bride, her brother, and I'm told driver of a seriously badass car today, Ethan Dessier."

God damn it, why didn't he drink something stronger than cran and soda! The next one was going to have vodka in it.

Regardless, he stepped to the podium.

"Thanks," he said, resisting the urge to clear his throat. He could show no weakness with this room full of people staring at him. "Many of you don't know me, and most days Arlene would tell you that's for the best." A murmur of giggles in the crowd. A decent, if not underwhelming start. Always lead with a joke. "She and I grew up not far from here. Children of the Windy City. And this is a wedding, so I'm not going to shi... uh, rain on it with stories of how unglamorous that upbringing was.

"However, this story doesn't happen without you knowing that there were bad times. Times you wouldn't wish on your worst enemy. Times we spent *with* our worst enemy, actually. Arlene and I were in it together, united against the world.

"That is, until she skipped town and left me."

Some laughter. Mostly of the nervous variety.

"It's ok, it's ok," he insisted. "She made a choice, and I'm here to tell you it was the right one. One I wish I'd made sooner, because maybe then I'd be a better person, or at least one as good as she is." He caught his sister's eyes and smiled. For a terrible public speaker, he was nailing it!

"Why is this important? Because when she told me she was getting married, and was willfully going to include me in the day for some reason, I didn't have a single reservation about it. I knew, from those early days when we went to waterparks, to the later ones where she rushed to my side after I had a... um... unfortunate run-in with a larger body of water, that she was an amazing person whose heart made the right choices, even if they don't make sense at the time. Even if they hurt.

"So, from that, I know Matthew is the right man for her, because she would never be here if she wasn't sure. If she wasn't completely positive. Because Arlene, more than anybody I know..." he looked at his sister again. There were certainly tears there.

But then, he looked at Victoria, who was watching him intensely, and he held her eyes with everything he had in his heart. "...she knows that love is about making the hard choices."

Jesus, did he just choke up saying that? What a disgrace to all the Deaths that came before him. Somewhere a squirrel was vomiting forcefully.

Victoria, however, turned bright red.

Check. Mate.

Okay okay, wrap it up, shithead. "So please, raise your glass, and join me in a toast: to the bride Arlene, the most honest, most dedicated, most amazing, greatest sister who ever abandoned me."

Smiles in the crowd all around. It seemed they understood who Ethan was by this point. The glasses all raised.

Later, Ethan was as good as his word and behaved himself. The occasional snarky remark, but nothing critical. He had the first dance with Arlene, who took the opportunity to constantly whisper, "I hate you, I hate you, I hate you, look what you did to my makeup! I hate you, I hate you..." much to his delight before he passed her over to her new husband.

You think you hate me now, wait until you find out I put the Mustang keys in Matthew's pocket, sis...

And with that, Ethan's job was officially over.

It was easily the most successful wedding Death had ever been a part of.

Ethan was back at the bar he started at, red signature drink in his hand, when Victoria came over and sat next to him.

"I'll have what he's having," she said to the bartender with a smile.

"Careful," he warned, "they're addictive. Would you believe I actually put vodka in mine this time?"

She leaned against him, their mutual outfits complimenting one another perfectly, and they sipped their drinks together.

"That was a great speech," she told him. "You totally nailed it."

"Thanks. I thought so too! I hope to god I never have to do that again. I hate speaking in public."

"Who would have thought that Death was an anti-social outcast who wasn't good at human interaction. It simply doesn't make sense."

He laughed and she joined him. It was still fresh to her, the news and the scope of everything that he was. The images he'd shown her. The feelings, good and bad, he'd helped her experience.

In the end all he could be was honest. Completely honest.

And in the end, that was enough.

"So how come you worked so hard to avoid me before the wedding?" he asked, changing the subject away from his awkward profession. "I was sweating bullets looking for you."

She smiled at him. "And miss the chance to see your face when you walked in and looked at my dress? Not on your life."

"Oh whatever. You have no idea what I was looking at. I was wearing sunglasses! I was actually checking out that JP. She was older, but she could bring it!"

She punched him in the leg. "Whatever. I crushed it and you know it."

He agreed. "You did. You look fantastic. I recommend a bit of black, though. It pulls it all together."

The mischievous look she gave him was devastating. "Oh I'm wearing black. Trust me." *Sound the alarms! We can't take this kind of pressure anymore!* "Honestly, you look great, too. I like this color on you. Like, a lot."

Something was bugging him and he had to ask. Again, he had to resist the urge to just check the background of the universe to find out. Human interaction would likely never be easy for him. "How did you do it? How did you know I'd be wearing this?"

Her wry smile was heartwarming. "I pivoted. I honestly had another outfit picked out and everything! But when I saw that picture..." They both drifted off, thinking of Laurel's drawing fondly. "... anyway, I asked Arlene if I could make a change. I even told her I was pretty sure it was what you were going to wear. Glad to see I was right."

"Yeah, but, how? Honestly? Was it just a guess?"

She took a sip, and then looked at him. "Let's just call it fate."

He rolled his eyes, and meant every movement of it from the very bottom of his heart.

More silence for a moment as they soaked in the scene around them, of happy couples both old and new. Rachelle and one of the groomsmen were all over each other in the corner. It made them both laugh.

"Well, mission accomplished I suppose," Ethan said eventually. She looked at him questioningly. He elaborated. "When Arlene asked me to do this, I surmised that my role would be to give Matthew some cheesy advice, hand her over, and then get tanked and fuck a bridesmaid."

She mocked being insulted. "Huh! What the hell gives you that idea, you shit?"

He shrugged. "Wishful thinking, I guess. Can't blame a guy for his horribly impure, and frankly scandalous, thoughts."

She stepped from the bar and moved in front of him, taking Ethan's hands while kissing him deeply. "Maybe not so wishful."

He blushed and he knew it. His cheeks undoubtedly matched their ensemble.

"Say it again," she asked. "Say it only to me."

At first he wasn't sure what she meant, but then it clicked. The room faded away from their periphery and it was just the two of them.

"Love is about making the hard choices."

Her eyebrow raised again, and again he was helpless. "Is that what this is?"

Be honest, don't be an ass, be honest, don't be an ass...

Be honest.

"Yes. That's what this is. The first part, anyway. The rest is actually easy, *because* of the first part. That's actually the trick."

She kissed him again, and their eyes met.

"I completely agree."

Beyond the bustle, when no one noticed them and the energy and joy of the party consumed the masses in the kind of euphoria only pure happiness can bring, Ethan and Victoria faded effortlessly into the night.

EPILOGUE

Laurel died two days after Arlene's wedding, as Ethan guessed she would. Laurel had to see it through. That was her role in this. Her will knew she couldn't win against the enemy that was killing her, but she could last until she was satisfied that the world she was leaving behind was a better one for everyone she loved.

She was a shell of even the woman Ethan had first met when the end came, but he learned long before that moment that who we are when we left this world was rarely if ever who we were when we lived in it at our peak. He never knew her pre-cancer, but he was thankful for the Laurel he did get to know all the same.

He even had the privilege of being there when the moment came, not as Death, but as Ethan. He'd barely met their parents, but when both Laurel and Victoria told them how much it would mean to them both to have him there, and considering the nature of his and Vic's new relationship, they agreed.

When they knew the moment was coming, surrounded by other friends and family as well, there wasn't a dry eye in the room.

Except Ethan.

His previously stoic ability to never cry had been fractured a number of times by this point, but this was different. This was a woman who knew what she was facing and did so willingly, with no reservations. Much like the unfortunate Dotty before her, Laurel knew how to "die right".

She passed away peacefully, holding both her sister and her

mother's hands, Ethan standing in the back, giving the family their moment.

Ethan the Entity of Death, however, was right there with her. A part of him felt that she knew he was there and was thankful for it. As she passed, life escaped her as it did with everyone and everything, and he placed every light exactly where it belonged in the glory of the beyond, and he was honored he had the opportunity to do so.

He absolutely painted the stars with her light.

And while he was there, he fixed the rip, closing the connection he had with her. That hurt the most, he thought.

And those in the room cried, because that was natural. There had to be pain when you said goodbye to someone; otherwise, what was the point of ever being together in the first place?

Once the professionals who had been waiting in the wings monitoring the moment were finally allowed in to begin removing her, and Victoria had stopped hugging her parents and consoling one another together to allow them the chance to follow the process with their other daughter, Vic came back to Ethan and hugged him tightly while the rest of those in attendance said their piece.

Weddings and deaths. The two great unifiers.

Ethan held her, the human part of him wishing he could take her pain away, but the professional part of him knowing the pain was needed. He admitted that his human side felt the pain as well. It was nice having a friend to talk about the things he saw and had to deal with. Once again, when it came to being Death and all the confusing emotions that brought with it, he was alone.

As if on cue, Victoria hugged him tighter.

Well, not completely alone.

Later in the day, before her parents came home, Victoria and Ethan were sitting on the back deck, looking over the lake. Much like the wedding, it was a beautiful day.

She hadn't said more than two words to him since Laurel's last breath. He felt he knew what was coming, once she had the courage to ask. And then it came.

"How did it go?"

Honesty, the best policy, and this time it was thankfully easy. "Perfectly. Every bit in the right place."

She stuttered, but didn't stop. "And the rip?"

"Fixed. No longer a problem."

"How did you fix it?"

That was more complicated. He knew he wanted every part of Laurel to go where it belonged. In the end he had met a wonderful older hummingbird set to pass away at the same time who, through their strange means of communication, agreed to help fix the rip.

After he explained it, Vic smiled. "She loved hummingbirds. She always filled the yard with feeders."

"Yeah, I suspect that was why it was willing to help. I'd never tried asking before. I'd just fixed the problem as best I could. I learned something today."

More silence, but Ethan was now a trained expert in keeping his mouth shut. Whenever he opened it, things tended to come out without parental supervision.

She reached over and took his hand. "Thank you. For… whatever it is you did, thank you."

"It was honestly my pleasure."

The wind blew and the deck was warm. "Even with everything I know now, even with everything you showed me, it still hurts."

Ethan knew the feeling very well. "The pain is how you know it was worth it."

The funeral was wonderful, and soon after, Laurel's celebration of life was a party and a half. Whoever she was before cancer laid her low;

she was apparently worth celebrating enthusiastically. At least for the people loyal enough to see her through the darkest times.

The party bustling around them, Ethan joined Victoria in what had been Laurel's room. It had been cleaned and organized, but it was still the same room. Little had changed.

Victoria walked to the bedside table and removed the book of drawings. "Do these rips still happen?" she asked.

Ethan nodded. "Yeah. They never stopped. There was a hard one yesterday."

"I'm sorry to hear that. A part of me wished something in her passing would magically end them."

Ethan agreed. "That would have been great, but it wasn't her place in this. This is my problem to fix. It always was. But hey, learning that things can help, like that hummingbird, has opened all new possibilities. I'm still exploring them."

Victoria passed the book to Ethan. "She wanted you to have this."

"What? No. No way. Those should be yours, or your parents. I was there, I don't need them."

"Yeah, she thought you'd say that. She wrote a note for you on the last page. Proof positive that they're yours."

Ethan slumped. "Well shit," he took the book. "Don't I feel like hot garbage. Seriously, these should be yours."

She smiled softly at him. "And am I going anywhere? It's not like I won't ever see them again."

"No," he agreed, "that's true. Not unless you want to get away from me."

"No. Not at all."

"Good," he declared, casually opening the book, looking over the shared adventures, "because my stalking abilities are basically unstoppable these days." *Too far, dumbass!* "I'm kidding."

"Kidding? Why do you think I do that thing with my breasts when I get out of the shower? I just assume you're watching me. Frankly, I'm upset you haven't said anything. It's sexy as hell."

Flaming. Hot. Red. Face. "Uh… but I… you know I wouldn't…"

"Oh well, opportunity missed." She winked. "Glad to know you're not being creepy."

God damned women. Seriously. Just the worst.

He let it pass and decided to open the last page of the book. No time like the present.

There was no drawing. Just a message.

"Ethan, you had better look after her with everything you've got. Because if you don't, I will fucking kill you. Believe me. I know a guy. Thanks for everything, Laurel."

How the fuck did she know these words? Did she see him? Did Victoria hear them and tell her? No, he made damn sure it was just Matthew who heard them. And now Laurel was gone and he could never get an answer of how it was possible.

Unsurprisingly, the universe still had a few more secrets for him to discover.

"Satisfied?" Victoria asked.

"Never. Satisfaction is the first step to laziness."

"Well," she answered, "then we better just keep moving. Care to buy a girl a drink?"

"Of course. Where are you thinking?"

"Paris?"

Ethan smiled. What was the point of all this power if you didn't enjoy it once or twice? "For sure. I know a place."

With a look around to make sure the other guests didn't see, and with a quick double-check in the ether to make sure no cameras or prying eyes could see them, they vanished once more.

Paris at night was one of the true wonders of the world. With Victoria dressed to the nines, and Ethan dressed as... well, as Ethan, they enjoyed their nightcap while they took in the city.

"And you can come and go any time you like?" she asked, still amazed.

"Yes. Well, sorta. Remember, mirrors and all that. It's complicated."

"Right. And the universe doesn't get mad at your galivanting around with me?"

"I don't think I've ever heard someone unironically use 'galivanting' in a sentence before."

She shot a dirty look. "Oh whatever, you know what I mean."

He smiled back. "No, it's fine. It's just my life. I just happened to bring you along for the ride."

She raised her glass. "And I appreciate it." Her eyes looked around the view again, but then stopped as they looked just over his left shoulder. "Hey, isn't that..."

He was so wrapped up in the moment, and the beauty of the company, that he didn't even see her freeze. "Sorry, isn't that what?" Then he noticed her, glass still half in the air. "...What? What is it? Are you okay?"

She wasn't moving. Nothing was moving.

Everything everywhere was frozen.

"I gotta tell ya, kid, even at the best of our times together, I never saw this beauty coming."

That voice. That memorable, horrible, punchable voice.

Slowly, and with as much restraint as he could muster, Ethan turned around.

Sitting at the table behind them, a steaming coffee in his hand, was a tall, pale man, hair sun-bleached blonde, dressed all in perfectly matching black. A terrible knit sweater with three-quarter length sleeves, black pleather pants, and black Air Force 1s.

The man cocked an eyebrow at the stunned Ethan and his immotile date. "You picked a fucking winner there, no doubt about it. Tell me, as the first Death ever to have sex, was it amazing? I'll bet it was amazing. Some really freaky shit no doubt."

Ethan couldn't even speak.

"What's the matter? Squirrel got your tongue?"

"You. Sonnuva. Bitch."

The man leaned back, feigning being wounded. "Oh, that's not fair. I think you'd win in that category, sport. Had any blueberry muffins lately?"

"No," Ethan spit out. "I keep them in the dark where they fucking belong."

The man's smile faded. "I believe you."

"What are you doing here? Better, how? No, even better, fuck off!"

He held his hands up defensively. "Hey, I would if I could! But I've got a job to do, and I'm afraid I don't get much say in the matter."

"What job?"

That smile. That horrible smile. "Why, helping you, of course."

Ethan didn't reply, but his eyes screamed "explain". The man got the message. He wasn't Death, not anymore, because that was Ethan now. So who or what was he?

"I've been sent to help with your little problem. Shepard you once more to the universe's final goal: balance. See, you fucked that up, and although you're doing better than I would have thought you were capable of trying to fix it, it's not enough. You need a boost."

"The fuck I do. I've been Death longer than you were even alive as a fucking squirrel."

"That's true, yet here I am." He checked his watch, a gawdy black Swatch that looked like it was from the eighties. "Look, I've got a couple other things to look after before we get right into it and figure out why you're triggering all this trouble. I just wanted to pop in and say hi and ogle your lady friend there for a moment. I'll leave you two lovebirds alone. Try not to think of me when you're getting down and dirty."

And then, before he vanished into the night, the three words Ethan feared more than any other came from the man's stupid lips.

"See you soon."

Time suddenly rushed forward again, catching up to its regular pace. Ethan just sat, stunned. The seat where the man had been sitting was empty now.

"Ethan. Ethan!" it was Victoria.

He looked back, dazed. "I'm sorry, what?"

She looked at the empty seat behind him. "I said, isn't that the guy from Laurel's drawing? Your old 'boss' or whatever he was? But it's weird, he's gone now. I thought I saw someone that looked like him. He must have just left."

Ethan looked around. He even probed the cosmos looking for some sign of that jerk. Nothing. No sign anywhere.

"No," he said, eventually turning back to his girlfriend while he tried to hide his unbridled rage. "I think I saw who you meant. That wasn't him.

"That was just some asshole."

ABOUT THE AUTHOR

Marc Watson is an author of genre fiction of all lengths and styles. His debut novel *Death Dresses Poorly* was released in 2017, and you can find stories in his science-fantasy Ryuujin World in *Catching Hell: Journey* and *Catching Hell: Destination* (all from Fluky Fiction) as well as the short story collection *Between Conversations: Tales From the World of Ryuujin*.

Marc lives in Calgary, Alberta, Canada. He is a husband to a very patient wife and a proud father of two. He is an avid outdoorsman, baseball player, martial artist, poutine aficionado, and lover of all Mexican foods.

He can be found at online http://www.marcwatson.ca, as well as on Facebook at http://www.facebook.com/marcwroteabook, and on all other social media at @writewatson

www.ingramcontent.com/pod-product-compliance
Lightning Source LLC
Chambersburg PA
CBHW031348170626
46807CB00002B/877